*JONATHAN GOES WEST*

*by the same author*

THE BLACK BUCCANEER

LONGSHANKS

RED HORSE HILL

AWAY TO SEA

LUMBERJACK

WHO RIDES IN THE DARK?

T-MODEL TOMMY

BOY WITH A PACK

CLEAR FOR ACTION!

BLUEBERRY MOUNTAIN

SHADOW IN THE PINES

THE SEA SNAKE

THE LONG TRAINS ROLL

JONATHAN GOES WEST

BEHIND THE RANGES

RIVER OF THE WOLVES

CEDAR'S BOY

WHALER 'ROUND THE HORN

BULLDOZER

THE FISH HAWK'S NEST

SPARKPLUG OF THE HORNETS

THE BUCKBOARD STRANGER

GUNS FOR THE SARATOGA

SABRE PILOT

EVERGLADES ADVENTURE

THE COMMODORE'S CUP

THE VOYAGE OF THE JAVELIN

WILD PONY ISLAND

BUFFALO AND BEAVER

SNOW ON BLUEBERRY MOUNTAIN

PITTSBURG

# Jonathan Goes West

*by* *STEPHEN W. MEADER*

ILLUSTRATED BY EDWARD SHENTON

ISBN 978-1-931177-12-2 cloth
ISBN 978-1-931177-13-9 paperback

SOUTHERN SKIES

LITTLE ROCK, ARKANSAS

www.southernskies.com

*Dedication*

*The republication of this book is dedicated with love to Jim Long by his best friend, Jerry Atchley.*

## *LIST OF ILLUSTRATIONS*

*JONATHAN GOES WEST*

# *ONE*

THE ROOSTER CROWED AGAIN, AND JONATHAN STIRRED IN THE deep old featherbed. There was a cloud of trouble on his mind as he came out of his half-sleep, but it was a moment or two before he remembered. Then he sat up, rubbing his eyes, and blinked at the pale, pink light of dawn coming through the gable window.

This was the last day. Tomorrow he would be leaving.

The thought lay like a hard green apple at the pit of his stomach.

Jonathan got up and pulled on his barn clothes—the old, stained butternut breeches and linsey-woolsey shirt and the home-made cowhide boots. As he clumped down the stairs he could hear Aunt Polly starting the kitchen fire. Those homely sounds—the clink of the stove lid and the crackle of kindling in the flames—made his heart heavier than ever. He stole out through the entry way, doused his head at the pump, and went on to the barn.

It was going to be a nice day, he could see. One of those cool, clear, sparkling days that come to Maine in the late spring. The grass, released from the long grip of frost, was a fresh, vivid green against the dull red of the barn door.

Inside, in the warm half darkness, there was a pleasant murmur of sound. Along one side of the dim floor rose the haymow. On the other he could see the heads of the animals, peering out between their stanchions. First the two horses, then the big black-and-white oxen, and beyond them the long line of cows. They drew deep, contented sighs, clicked their horns, rustled the fodder in the mangers and chewed steadily, rhythmically.

The boy took a clean wooden milk pail from the shelf and picked up a three-legged stool. He went through the doorway leading from the barn floor to the rear of the stalls.

A spare, stoop-shouldered man with iron-gray hair

crouched on a stool by the flank of the first cow, wiping her teats before starting to milk. He looked up and smiled.

"Morning, Jon."

"Morning, Uncle Eli."

He knew his voice sounded hollow, but it was hard to put any real enthusiasm into the greeting on such a day.

Uncle Eli shot a quick glance at him from keen gray eyes, then bent his head against the cow's flank.

"So-o-o, boss," he muttered, and the first jets of milk drummed loud in the bottom of the pail.

Jonathan went to the other end of the tie-up. Old Daisy looked around at him with mild-eyed reproof as he pushed her over to make room for his stool. She must have sensed the unhappiness in his touch, but she let down her milk without fidgeting.

The sun was up when the last milk pail had been filled and carried into the cool cellar. The boy and his uncle washed and sat down at the table in the big kitchen.

Aunt Polly set the bowlfuls of steaming oatmeal before them and paused for a second by Jonathan's chair. She laid a hand lightly on his shoulder. Somehow it made him feel better. He managed a smile.

"Good morning, Aunt Polly," he said.

She took the chair opposite her husband's and they bowed their heads in a silent grace. When he looked at her again he saw his own trouble reflected in her understanding eyes.

"It's going to be a fine day, Eli," she said. "I expect Jon would like some time to himself. You'll be plowing, and I must mend his things and pack them."

Uncle Eli nodded. "Soon as the chores are done, you can go where you like, lad. I still can't understand it, though. Most boys your age'd be counting the hours till they could start such a trip."

Jonathan didn't lift his eyes. He swallowed another spoonful of porridge before he spoke.

"I'm not scared of the trip," he said quietly. "It's going away from here—maybe forever. Never seeing the farm again—or the lake—or Aunt Polly and you."

"Shucks!" Uncle Eli answered. "I shouldn't wonder if there's prettier places out in that western country. Shorter winters, too. And easier farming. They tell me there isn't a stone in miles o' that black prairie. Plenty o' young folks have gone from 'round here. Why, look what that Greeley fellow keeps saying every week in the 'Tribune.' 'Go west, young man'—that's what he says."

Jonathan had no answer, for in that year of 1845 the weekly "New York Tribune" was already regarded as second only to the Bible by New England country people.

He finished his breakfast and went back to the barn. The slant sunlight glistened on the dewy grass. Out of the blue air overhead came a cascade of melody from a soaring bobolink. Somewhere in the old orchard across the road a lamb bleated and its mother answered.

The boy turned the cattle into the barnyard and pumped water into the hollow-log troughs. When they had finished drinking he herded the cows across the road and into the lane that led uphill to the pasture. Then he returned and cleaned out the stalls, spreading fresh straw for bedding. He watered and curried the horses and fed the hens.

His uncle, meanwhile, had carried skimmed milk to the pigs and calves, set the wide, shallow crocks of cream to thicken for butter-making, and now was yoking up the oxen, ready to plow the south field.

The great, patient beasts stood chewing their cuds unconcernedly while the heavy yoke was laid across their necks and the hickory bows fastened in place. Jonathan helped hook the chain to the drag on which the plow rested.

Uncle Eli laid the goad gently against the shoulder of the nigh ox. "Gee up, Bright," he ordered. "Get along, Star."

Like a pair of sleepwalkers they heaved slowly forward till the chain drew taut, then lumbered off beside their master. The boy watched till they passed the big lilac bush at the roadside. At last he turned and went back to the rutted, grass-grown path that led down from the farm buildings to the lake.

The farm lay on the hillside like a long patchwork quilt, its upper end in the woods beyond Mt. Pisgah, its lower fields bordering the shore of Cobbosseecontee. This morning the water was blue and sparkling under the May sun.

Jonathan kicked off his boots and set off at a trot down the hill, his bare feet reveling in the moist coolness of the grass.

Deep in a grove of cedars by the rocky shore, his skiff lay bottom up on its rack of poles. It was a light, tough, little boat of cedar. Uncle Eli had helped him build it two winters before. He dragged the craft down to the water, took a pair of oars from under the thwart, where they had weathered the winter, and climbed in. Three or four quick strokes shot him out from the shore.

Cobbosseecontee meant "place of the sturgeon" in the old Indian tongue, though even Uncle Eli couldn't recall when such a fish had been caught there. Nearly ten miles from end to end and two miles wide, it lay among the hills like a slim blue sword. Islands, big and small, dotted its length. The water was deep and clear—so clear that Jonathan could see the bass and salmon moving along the stony bottom, forty feet below.

He paddled across to Upper Sister Island and pulled the little boat out on a sloping granite ledge under the fringe of pines. The sun lay warm on the rock and he sat there for half an hour, storing up the beauty of the place he loved.

A mile away on the hillside he could see the rambling white house, connected by sheds to the big red barn—the checkerboard of fields and orchards climbing to the rocky pasture—and off to the south, the black-and-white dots of the oxen, moving slowly along the line between green grass and brown tillage.

Why couldn't he stay here, where he had spent twelve of his sixteen years? He had to choke back a rising resentment against his father. It was hard to feel any affection for a man who had written only two or three letters in all the time since his mother's death. Always Matthew Brent had been a wanderer. When he departed, leaving his small son in charge of his brother, Eli, more than five years had passed before they heard from him. Then a letter had come from a place called Buffalo, in New York State. He had been to Europe and around the Horn in a clipper ship—settled for a brief time in Canada—worked on the Erie Canal as purser of a packet-boat.

The next time he wrote it was from Cincinnati, on the Ohio River, where he had been dealing in real estate. And finally, after another long silence, had come last month's letter. Jonathan winced as he thought of it. His father had taken a half-section of Illinois prairie land and was going back to farming.

"Now that the boy is big enough to be some help," the message had read, "I think it is time for us to give him a home. There will be more work on the new farm than I can manage alone, and we expect to have a school here next year. My interest in Grandfather Crocker's place ought to be worth $500 or more. You can sell it for whatever you can get and have Jonathan bring me the money, which I need for a team of horses and other equipment. My wife and self are well and hope this finds you the same."

Jonathan knew the contents of the letter by heart, and even now that reference to "my wife" made him wince. He felt an instinctive dislike for the stepmother he had never seen.

He rowed back across the lake, rippling now in a playful breeze. Carefully he replaced the skiff and started up the hill once more. This time he didn't stop at the house. He climbed the length of three fields and went over the stone wall into the high pasture. Ahead of him the granite ledges rose like giant stairs to the summit of Mt. Pisgah. The sun on the hilltop brought out the fragrant smell of sweet fern and pennyroyal growing in chinks of the rocks. Stooping he picked the tender leaves of checkerberry and nibbled on them as he climbed.

At last he was on the highest ledge, with the farm and the lake spread out at his feet. Forty miles to the west loomed Mt. Blue and Saddleback. And in the cleft between Saddleback's twin humps was the gleaming white peak of Mt. Washington, a hundred miles away in New Hampshire.

He could see the cows grazing in the pasture below and the young lambs frisking in the orchard, where apple blossoms were beginning to show pink. Halfway down the hill was the tumbled section of wall where the old woodchuck lived. He had stalked the wily animal for years, first with his bow and arrow, then with the ancient smooth-bore gun that Great-Grandfather Crocker had used to fight Indians.

It looked as if the woodchuck could live out his life in peace now, for Uncle Eli was too busy to bother him.

Over behind the hilltop were the dark, mysterious woods —hemlock and pine and hackmatack—stretching away toward the Kennebec. With his uncle he had spent many a snowy day in the forest, cutting winter firewood or helping fell big trees to be hauled to the sawmill for boards. And a little to the south was the cutover land where he had picked blueberries and blackberries in summer and once had seen a bear.

Slowly he went down the hill, taking a farewell look at each landmark. Down in the dooryard, under the elms, Aunt Polly was busy with her trowel, planting seeds for her flower garden. A pleasant smell came from the kitchen.

"Gee, Aunt Polly," he murmured, "if it wasn't May I'd think that was a berry pie you're baking!"

She laughed. "Don't you remember all the quarts o' blueberries I canned last summer? I made a pie special for your dinner. If your nose was really sharp you'd know I've been frying doughnuts, too. I don't aim to have you go hungry the first few days o' your trip, anyhow."

At noon, Uncle Eli drove the oxen into the yard and unyoked them. "Reckon that's all the plowing we'll do today," he said. "This afternoon I aim to churn. I'll carry a load o' butter down when I take you to the river tomorrow."

Dinner, that day, was something of a feast. Aunt Polly had cooked her famous chicken and dumplings and set out four or five kinds of pickles and preserves. There were hot biscuits, too, and blueberry pie, and big glasses of cold, rich milk.

When the dishes were cleared away, Uncle Eli went down cellar. The patent churn was his pride and joy. Instead of standing upright and working with an up-and-down plunger, it lay on its side on four legs, and a crank turned the wooden paddles inside.

It was damp and cool in the deep stone cellar, with a mossy smell like the bottom of a well. Jonathan watched his uncle take the cream off the tops of the crocks with a broad, perforated skimmer—cream so thick it lifted like a golden blanket from the surface of the milk.

"Jon," said his uncle, looking at the thermometer on the wall, "it's just a mite warm down here for churning. S'pose you get a chunk of ice."

The ice-house stood in a shaded north corner behind the barn. Each winter it was filled with cakes of clear ice, two feet thick, that they cut themselves on the lake. Packed in sawdust, the precious stuff lasted all through the summer.

The boy dug through the sawdust, hacked off a fifty-pound piece of ice with the ax, and carried it to the cellar. His uncle let the cream jar stand in a nest of cracked ice for a few minutes before pouring it into the churn. Then began the rhythmic turning of the crank. Jonathan took the first part of the job. He liked to hear the soft *slap-slap* of the cream against the sides of the churn.

Uncle Eli stood by, his head cocked like a sparrow's, listening. After a short time he nodded and motioned his nephew out of the way. He could tell by the sound that the butter had started to come. The noise it made now was deeper—a sort of *chunk-chunk.*

"Call your Aunt Polly," he told the boy.

She came down in a moment, drying her hands on her apron. "Making" the butter was her task. It was taken from the churn—a great golden mass as big as a peck measure—and placed on a fresh-scrubbed table top. There Aunt Polly kneaded it back and forth with a grooved rolling-pin, working in the salt by measured handfuls, while her husband drained off the buttermilk from the bottom of the churn. As soon as the butter was evenly flavored, Jonathan shaped it in a round wooden mold, leaving the imprint of a carved strawberry and leaves on the top of each half-pound pat. That mold—the Brent trade-mark—was famous in the Kennebec Valley country. Well-to-do housewives prided themselves on having Brent butter on their tables.

When the boy finished there were thirty pounds—sixty perfect pats—stored neatly on racks in a wooden box, ready for their trip to market.

"Well," said Uncle Eli, looking at his big silver watch, "it's getting near chore time. We'll all turn in early tonight so we can make an early start. Cap'n Foster's schooner sails at eight-thirty, an' it's eleven miles to Gardiner."

# TWO

PRINCE, THE GOOD BAY TROTTER, WAS PAWING HOLES IN THE new grass of the dooryard when Jonathan came out at seven o'clock. Aunt Polly's arm was around his squared shoulders. With no children of her own she loved him like her own son.

She shed no tears at parting. "Write to me, Jon," was all she said, and her smile was brave and bright.

The boy stowed his portmanteau under the seat of the spring wagon and turned to kiss her.

"I'll write," he said. "And some day I'm coming back."

Blinking a little he climbed hastily into the wagon, and

Uncle Eli clucked to the horse. When the boy looked back, his aunt was still standing under the elms, shading her eyes with her hand and waving good-bye.

"Going to be another nice day for the start o' your trip," Uncle Eli remarked. "Good thing I got Prince shod last week. We got to step along if we're to get you there 'fore the schooner sails."

The wagon had an open bed behind the seat, and there the butter box rode in a larger chest, packed with ice. In spite of the weight he pulled, Prince stepped out eagerly on the rolling dirt road. Half a mile from home they went over the crest of Meeting-House Hill, and started down the slope beyond. Jonathan craned his neck to get a last glimpse of the lake before the pines hid it from view.

They drove through the crossroads hamlet known as the "Forks," and headed for the river. It was quarter to eight by the town clock when they went down the last steep pitch into Hallowell.

"Reckon I'd better lighten the load," said Uncle Eli. He stopped in front of a store on the main street, and Jonathan helped him lift the chest out on the high platform.

"Watch it, will you, Jeff?" he called to the storekeeper. "I'll be back, soon's I hustle the boy down to Gardiner."

The road along the river bank was level and hard. Uncle Eli lifted the reins a little and spoke to the horse, and they flashed out of the Hallowell streets and into green country.

Jonathan always caught his breath when he saw the Kennebec. Running broad and deep between its hills, it was a king of rivers—a highway linking Maine with all the world. Above the falls it was filled now almost from bank to bank with floating logs that had been rafted down on the spring freshets. Below were shipyards, scattered along the shore from Hallowell to Bath. And the commerce of the river—its lumber and fish and potatoes—traveled the seven seas in Kennebec-built hulls.

The bay trotter's ears pricked up as he sighted a buggy on the road ahead. Uncle Eli chuckled. "Looks like Lawyer Scraggs' rig," he said. "Haven't had a brush with that gray nag o' his in years."

The wheels of the spring wagon spun faster and the dust whirled away in clouds behind them. When they had pulled up within forty yards, Jonathan saw a lean face peer out around the buggy top. Then a hand went out to seize the whip, and the gray horse leaped ahead under its sting.

For the next half mile Uncle Eli was satisfied to hold his position close behind the speeding buggy. But Prince wasn't content with that kind of race. He tossed his head, trying to get the bit in his teeth.

"Well," the farmer grinned, "here's a wide place in the road. Might as well take him now as any time."

He gave a sharp chirrup and pulled a little on the left rein. No other hint was needed. The bay stretched his neck and settled lower between the shafts, his flying feet thudding in quickened tempo. In a few seconds he was inching up past the buggy wheels—even with the gray.

Lawyer Scraggs gave them a venomous look from under his bushy eyebrows.

"Sorry," called Uncle Eli cheerfully. "Wouldn't want you to eat our dust, only we got to get to Gardiner 'fore the tide turns!"

He steadied the bay trotter when they were well ahead, and had him down to an easy road gait by the time the masts and steeples of Gardiner came into view.

"Eight-twenty she is, right on the dot," he announced, glancing at his watch. "Seven miles in thirty-five minutes, and old Prince has hardly got a good sweat up!"

They drove on through the middle of the bustling town and turned down a short, steep hill to the docks.

"There she lies," said Uncle Eli. "The *Phoebe Foster*. An' there's the skipper himself, acting like he was about ready to clear out, passenger or no passenger."

Jonathan saw a solidly built, ruddy-faced man striding up and down the pier. Grizzled curls showed from under his sea-cap, and he was puffing on a short black pipe.

"Ahoy, there!" he bellowed. "What's kept ye, Eli? Tide's at flood an' it's one bell o' the forenoon watch. I'd ha' given orders to cast off, only I knew ye was probably doin' yer best with that spavined hoss."

"Spavined, eh?" Uncle Eli shouted back at him. "Ask Lawyer Scraggs about this hoss. He's still trying to figure what passed him. Besides—it'll take you another hour to get sail on that rickety old tub o' yours!"

The two men grinned at each other and Uncle Eli reached out a hard, brown hand to grip the sailor's.

"Cap'n Foster," he said, "this is my nephew, Jonathan. He's your passenger. Reckon you won't have any trouble with him, for he's a pretty spry young sannup. Sort o' hate to see him go."

Jonathan shook the captain's hand. He was proud to be called a "sannup" by his uncle. It was a word that had come down from the Abenaki Indians—once lords of the Kennebec. It meant "young warrior."

Captain Foster was cordial. "Drop yer bag here on the dock," he said. "I'll have it carried aboard."

A seaman came and took the portmanteau, and the captain exchanged news with his old friend for a few minutes. Then he looked at his watch and roared out a command.

"Ready to cast off the for'ard moorin'!" he told the crew.

Uncle Eli shook hands with the skipper and gave Jonathan's shoulder a pat. "Keep your chin up, Jon," he said huskily. "An' don't forget you've got folks back here in Maine."

Then he turned quickly to the wagon, as Jonathan went aboard. He swung Prince around, waved once, and was gone up the hill.

"Let go aft," bellowed Captain Foster. "Stand by to h'ist the mains'l!"

As the halliards creaked through the sheaves and the snowy canvas shook out, Jonathan was suddenly aware of someone standing beside him. He looked into the laughing eyes of a girl about his own age. She had pretty brown hair, parted demurely in the middle and held by a net at the back of her neck. Her dress was of blue silk, slim-waisted and with the fashionable wide, ruffled skirt billowing outward about her feet. She wore a smart little fur-trimmed jacket, and her cheeks were rosy in the brisk May morning breeze.

"We may as well get acquainted," she smiled. "Father's too busy getting sail on to introduce us. I'm Prudence Foster, and we'll be fellow-passengers as far as Bath. I'm going down to visit at my aunt's. I suppose you're the Jonathan Brent I've heard so much about."

Jonathan reddened. He wasn't much used to stylish young ladies. "Yes," he managed to say. "That's my name. I'm pleased to meet you, Miss Foster."

"Let me show you the schooner," the girl suggested gaily. "She's not a very big ship but I know every inch of her. My brothers and I helped build her. That is—all I did was sort of superintend. That was five years ago and I wasn't big enough to saw timbers or swing a maul."

She led him forward to the bows and showed him the gilded figurehead under the jutting bowsprit.

"My Uncle Jabez carved it," she said. "It's supposed to look like Mother, only I think Mother's really a lot better-looking. The schooner's named for her, of course—*Phoebe Foster.* We've got a new kind of cargo this voyage. The whole lower hold is full of ice—a hundred tons of it—that Father's taking down to Baltimore. Folks around there will pay two or three cents a pound for good, clear Kennebec ice when the weather gets hot."

She showed him the crew's quarters in the forecastle, the chicken coop by the foremast, the trim little galley with its cookstove and provisions, and finally the cabins. A companionway just abaft the mainmast led down into a narrow room with a long table in the middle. Daylight came in through ports in the stern. Four smaller cabins opened off the sides. One belonged to Captain Foster, one to his son Abel, who acted as mate, and the other two were for Prudence and Jonathan.

"I shan't use mine this trip," she told him. "I'll be going ashore before night. But I've slept here often on other voyages. Father says he's taking you to New York. I wonder if you'll be seasick."

"Can't tell till I try," said Jonathan sheepishly. "I've never been to sea before."

She looked at him in surprise. "I suppose living back

there on the farm you wouldn't have much chance," she said. "All the boys I know in Gardiner go to sea. Some of them your age have been around the Horn, and one's a second mate on a clipper."

"I reckon we have other things to do," he said, a bit nettled. "If I was staying in Maine I'd like to sail before the mast, one voyage anyway. But I likely won't ever get to do it. I'm heading for Illinois."

"Oh," she replied, more respectfully. "That's a long way, isn't it? Aren't you afraid of Indians?"

He laughed. "From what I hear they cleared the Indians out o' that country quite a while back. It's wild enough, but it's supposed to be wonderful land to farm."

"How do you get there from New York?" the girl asked. "It must be hundreds of miles."

"That's right," said Jonathan. "Pretty near a thousand miles, I guess. When I get to New York, I've got a letter to Jeremiah Parsons, the merchant. He's a Maine man—came from Augusta and Uncle Eli used to know him. He'll get me passage on one of his schooners to Albany and I'll go by Erie Canal packet to Lake Erie. From there I'll try to get aboard a lake schooner going all the way to Chicago. Anyhow I ought to get as far as Sandusky or Detroit and I can travel by stage the rest of the way."

"My!" breathed Prudence. "Won't it take you months?"

"I hope to get there before the end of June," he answered.

"That way I'll be in time to help with the harvesting."

They went on deck again. With a westerly breeze abeam, the *Phoebe Foster* was running close-hauled down the middle of the broad river. Along both banks the hills rolled back—brown, tilled fields and vivid, green pastures, dotted with white farmsteads.

"Isn't it lovely?" said the girl impulsively. "I think I'd rather live on the Kennebec than anywhere else in the world!"

Jonathan made no answer, but she saw the bleak look in his eyes.

"Oh," she murmured. "That was thoughtless of me. I'm sorry."

They stopped at Richmond late in the morning to take aboard some additional freight. Dinner was served on deck at noon. The cook had made a kettle of real Maine clam chowder, steaming and rich, with milk, onions, fried salt pork and potatoes adding flavor to the succulent clams.

Jonathan ate two big bowls of chowder and topped them off with a spicy fried pie made of dried apples.

Another stop was made at Bowdoinham, and then they sailed out across Merrymeeting Bay. The wind still favored them but now the schooner was bucking a choppy head tide.

Captain Foster joined the two young people by the taffrail. "Won't be able to set ye ashore much before dark, I'm afraid," he told his daughter. "Too bad. Yer Aunt Ruth'll be in a swivet, I don't doubt."

Prudence laughed. "Aunt Ruth ought to understand about winds and tides after all these years," she said. "Anyhow, I don't mind a bit. I'll have more time with Jonathan."

They stood together by the high starboard rail and watched the sunset turn the mainsail to gold and pink. Prudence described some of her ocean voyages and Jonathan told her about the farm—the calf he had raised, his homemade skiff, and his camping trips on Horseshoe Island in Cobbosseecontee.

It was growing dark when the schooner neared the pier at Bath. Prudence's luggage had been brought on deck, and she waved a greeting to a well-dressed lady who sat in a carriage on shore.

"That's my aunt now," she said. "I'll have to hurry as soon as we're moored, so as not to keep her waiting any longer. But it's been fun, Jonathan. I wish I'd met you years ago instead of just today. I don't suppose I'll ever see you again, but I hope you get to Illinois safely."

She held out a firm young hand and he took it.

"Thanks, Prudence," he said. "I'll remember today for a long time. And some day I'm coming back."

They were the same words he had spoken to Aunt Polly, twelve hours before. He knew then that he meant them, and now he was surer than ever. It might be years, but he would return to this valley.

He watched the girl climb into the carriage, kiss her aunt, and then turn to wave a farewell before the high-stepping horses trotted away.

The boy felt lonesome for the first time. He watched the crew cast off and in a moment the *Phoebe Foster* was standing out into the harbor. Alongshore in the dusk he could see the tall hulls of half-built ships looming in their ways, and half a dozen big clippers lay at anchor in the channel. More than 80,000 tons of shipping were built in Bath in a year—a hundred full-rigged ships and brigs and coasting vessels. And they were the fastest, staunchest craft in all the world.

The night grew darker and the breeze freshened. The schooner held her way toward the sea. Under her forefoot the first slow heave of an ocean swell lifted her bowsprit toward the stars. Jonathan joined the skipper and mate in the cabin for supper.

"How's yer stomach, lad?" asked Captain Foster.

Jonathan grinned. "Must be all right so far," he said. "I'm hungry enough to eat a horse."

"Good boy," the captain laughed. "We'll make a sailor of you yet!"

# THREE

WHEN JONATHAN CAME ON DECK NEXT MORNING, THE schooner was rolling down the Gulf of Maine under full canvas. The day was cold and bright with a steady breeze still holding on the starboard beam.

He found his appetite was good for breakfast. And he forgot all about the motion of the ship in watching the taut sails and the blue rollers that came marching out of the west to crash in foam under the windward rail.

The skipper had the wheel himself that morning.

"It's prime sailin' weather," he told the boy. "We're loggin' close to eight knots. Ought to raise Truro on the Cape by noon."

Sure enough, before the cook called them to dinner there was a hail from the forward lookout. Off the starboard bow Jonathan could see a low gray haze of land and a tiny speck that Captain Foster said was a lighthouse.

They cruised down the shore of Cape Cod through the afternoon and skirted Nantucket Shoals before dark. The wind shifted in the night. Jonathan woke in his narrow berth to feel the violent pitching of the ship and hear shouts and running feet on the deck overhead. He pulled a blanket around him and stumbled to the companionway.

At the top of the steps he pulled open the sliding hatch and caught a douse of icy salt water full in the face. The deck was heeled far to starboard and huge, angry waves were breaking over the port rail. Looking aloft he saw that the foresail and fore-topsail had been taken in and the schooner was running under a reefed mainsail and a single storm jib.

The urgency had gone out of the captain's voice now. The orders he gave sounded calm enough, and Jonathan went back to his berth. But it was hours before he could get to sleep. Every timber in the schooner's sturdy hull creaked and groaned under the sea's buffeting.

When he woke it was gray daylight outside the tiny cabin

porthole. Lashed by the east wind the rain came scudding past. For the first time the boy had no desire to eat. He put on his boots and jacket and staggered out on deck for fresh air.

Captain Foster gave him a cheerful greeting. "Weather ain't quite as nice as it was," he said. "An' ye look a mite peaked this mornin'. East wind put ye off yer feed?"

"I'll be all right," Jonathan answered, hanging on to a shroud to keep from being blown away. "Where are we now, Captain?"

"Wal," grinned the older man, "it's sort o' hard to say. By dead reckonin' I'd put us somewhere sou'west o' Block Island. Soon's we get inside Montauk Point it ought to quiet down a bit. Anyhow the shift o' wind's givin' us a quick v'yage. We'd have had to beat our way in all the way from Nantucket if she'd stayed in the west. With luck we'll tie up in New York tomorrow mornin'."

By noon they had sighted the shore of Long Island to the south, and the waves were less boisterous. Captain Foster shook out the foresail and set another jib. With the wind still in the east, they bowled along up the Sound at a good clip. Jonathan's seasickness was gone now. After doing full justice to an excellent dinner he stood in the bows beside the lookout and watched for glimpses of land through the low, gray clouds.

"See that trail o' smoke to sta'board?" asked the sailor.

"That'll be the steam packet from New York headin' in fer New Haven. Dirty things—them steamboats!"

The schooner cut over toward the Connecticut shore late in the afternoon. The wind had been dropping steadily. At dusk it ceased altogether and a thick fog shut down. There was nothing for the skipper to do but strike sail and drop his anchor. A big seaman took his station at the bell amidships and began clanging out a warning at regular intervals. It was a lonesome, dreary sound, in those muffling shrouds of mist. Jonathan ate supper and curled up in his bunk. After a time he got used to the mournful tolling of the fog-bell, and the gentle heave of the swell rocked him to sleep.

When he woke again it was still dark outside, but he could hear footsteps and brisk orders and the noise of ropes being hauled. He dressed and went on deck. There was a little stir of breeze from the south. As the sun rose the mist began to swirl away and it was possible to see three or four hundred yards over the water.

A pair of seamen took hold of the capstan bars and pushed 'round and 'round, reeling in the cable. The anchor came up, weedy and dripping, and the sails were hauled aloft. Gracefully the schooner bowed to starboard and crisp little waves began to cream past under her lee.

The weather improved steadily all morning. The sun was bright on the green shore when they passed Stratford Point. An hour later smoke appeared on the horizon astern, and a steamer came puffing up the Sound, slowly overhauling them.

"He's only makin' about eight knots to our six," said the captain, squinting at the other craft. "He'll beat us in, but not by too much."

Shortly after noon the steamboat pulled up abeam, passing so near that Jonathan could see the splash of her side paddles and hear the clank and clatter of the big walking-beam, high up on her superstructure. Black smoke belched from her twin stacks. Raised, gilded letters on the paddle-boxes bore her name—"New York."

"Biggest steamboat on the Sound," growled Captain Foster. "Ain't really a ship, though. Wouldn't stay afloat an hour in a Cape Hatteras hurricane."

"What about the steam packets that go to England?" Jonathan asked. "They must run into some rough weather."

"Them? Oh, sure. But they're good stout sailin' ships with en-gines built into 'em." He pronounced the word as if it rhymed with "pines."

The waters narrowed gradually, with headlands jutting out from both shores. The boy saw occasional small, white-painted lighthouses perched on rocky islets. Then they were running into the jaws of a narrow channel where the tide boiled and eddied.

"Hell Gate," announced the skipper. "What ye might call the back door to New York. Dangerous place in a fog or a storm."

He spun the wheel dexterously and the schooner slipped through safely into calmer waters beyond. Shortly they were sailing past an island where oddly clad people hooted at them from behind the barred windows of a huge stone building.

"Who are they?" asked Jonathan, shocked at their antics.

"Loonies," Captain Foster grinned. "That's an insane asylum. Always holler an' cut up like that when a ship comes by. There's a jail on the island, too, an' a sort of a poorhouse, I guess you'd call it."

Soon the green fields along both shores of the East River gave way to shanties and fish houses. Then they could see the closely built-up streets of a city, overhung by smoke.

"That's New York," said the captain proudly. "Got more folks livin' in it than any town in these here United States! Over yonder, to port, is what they call Brooklyn. Look at them steam ferryboats scootin' across!"

Jonathan stood rooted to the deck, his mouth open in wonder. Never had he seen so many people, so many boats, so much bustling activity. The sun was near setting and its golden light struck the pine masts and spars and furled canvas of scores of tall ships that lined the docks. Drays rattled over the cobbles, dogs barked, bells rang and whistles tooted. Crowds of men and women came hurrying down out of the city's streets to board the ferries that would carry them home from work. There were big brick warehouses back of the docks, and beyond them towering buildings, five or six stories high—the counting-houses of merchants and bankers. Highest of all were the church spires. There seemed to be dozens of them, and now their bells were ringing the hour. First one, then another, then several together clanged out the seven notes—some deep, some high and clear, but all blending in a kind of stately music that made the farm boy shiver with delight.

The captain steered close to the end of one of the wharves. Cupping his hands he shouted something to a man on the pierhead and got an answer.

"Slack the main sheet!" the skipper roared. "Sta'board yer helm. Stand by in the bows there, an' look alive to moor her."

The schooner glided neatly in alongside the dock and a sailor heaved a cable from the deck forward. In a moment the craft was made fast fore and aft and her sails were being furled.

"There we are," Captain Foster chuckled. "Got ye safe to New York, son. Too late now to pay yer visit to old Parsons, though. His office closed up an hour ago. You better sleep aboard here an' go see him in the mornin'."

The evening was warm, and after supper Jonathan sat on the cabin coaming for hours, fascinated by the sights and sounds of the town. As it grew darker, a man with a little ladder and a long, flickering taper came down a near-by street. There were half a dozen lamp-posts scattered along the dockside, and he stopped at each in turn, climbing up, turning on the gas and lighting the jet. It was a strange sight to the Maine boy, used to whale-oil lamps.

An occasional tipsy sailor came out of a grog-shop, singing lustily and weaving his way over the cobblestones. Once the watch passed by on his rounds. He carried a stout staff and a bull's-eye lantern that he flashed into dark corners along the docks.

The chugging ferryboats still shuttled across the East River at intervals. After the moon rose Jonathan could see a tall ship moving slowly up from the lower bay under shortened sail. She towed a little yawl astern—a craft which one of the seamen on watch explained was the pilot-boat.

It was late when the boy turned in, but he slept soundly, lulled by the gentle cluck and gurgle of the tide around the piling.

The noises of the waking city roused him. The bells and whistles resumed their clamor and there was a great barking and snarling of dogs, punctuated by squeals and grunts that could only come from a pig. Hurrying on deck he saw a battle royal in progress on the waterfront.

Two huge, gaunt hogs, that had been scavenging for scraps along the dockside, were fighting off the onslaught of a pack of stray curs.

"Don't they keep their pigs penned up around here?" Jonathan asked the skipper.

"Shucks, no!" he laughed. "If it warn't fer them, the streets'd git so foul ye couldn't live in 'em. The butchers throw their offal out in the gutter, an' the hogs an' dogs clean it up. Nobody owns 'em. They jest roam around wild like."

After breakfast the boy brought his bag on deck and prepared to take his leave of the schooner.

"Ye've been a first-class passenger an' I hate to see ye go," said the captain heartily. "Parsons' countin'-house is jest up yonder on Broadway. Ye'll find it easy enough. Got yer money safe, have ye?"

"Yes, sir!" Jonathan told him. "Uncle Eli made me a money-belt out of an old harness strap, and Aunt Polly sewed a buckskin pouch onto it. All the money and my father's letter to Uncle Eli are in that. Nobody can get it without undressing me!"

"Good 'nough," said the skipper. "Well, we'll be unloadin' here today, if ye need any help or advice. But I reckon ye'll be halfway to Albany by nightfall. A good v'yage to ye! Come back to Maine some time."

They shook hands and Jonathan tossed his bag to the dock and jumped ashore. Waving farewell to the genial captain, he squared his shoulders and set off alone on the next stage of his long journey.

Young clerks were sweeping off the steps of office buildings and rolling up the shutters. Heavy drays and farmers' wagons from Long Island jostled each other in the narrow streets. Teamsters shouted, whips cracked and horses snorted. Behind him he heard a patter of small hoofs and looked around to see a drover guiding a flock of sheep up from the waterside. The principal streets were paved from curb to curb with stone, but some of the lanes and byways he passed were morasses of black mud.

Broadway was easy to recognize when he reached it. The width of the famous thoroughfare amazed him. There was room for half a dozen vehicles to pass abreast. Hotels and office buildings and tall, elegant residences of brick and brownstone lined it on either side.

Already there was heavy traffic moving. He saw a four-horse mail coach pull out for the north, with passengers waving gaily from their seats inside and on top. The coachman blew a great blast on his horn and cracked the whip smartly over the rumps of the lead team, and they swung out at a trot into the tide of carts and carriages.

Ladies dressed in the height of fashion went tripping along the sidewalks, bound for market. Behind each one came a servant carrying a huge basket to hold the provisions.

The country boy stood goggle-eyed, watching all these sights. It was ten minutes later that he remembered he had an important errand. Looking at the numbers on the doorposts he moved slowly northward another block. Then he caught sight of gilt letters on a black signboard. "Jeremiah Parsons, Merchandise Forwarded," it read.

He climbed the marble steps, then a flight of wooden stairs inside. Gingerly he opened the office door on the landing. A scrawny-looking clerk got down from his high stool, stuck his pen behind his ear and came to the gate, bowing to the visitor. Then he took another look at the boy's country clothes and his servile manner changed at once.

"Well?" he asked, with a bored air.

"I have a letter to Mr. Parsons," Jonathan explained. "Is he here?"

The clerk shook his head. "You won't see him today, my lad," he replied condescendingly. "He's away on business."

He turned on his heel and went back to his tall desk.

"You—you mean he'll be back tomorrow?" asked Jonathan, upset by the news.

"He might be here tomorrow." The man scowled. "I couldn't say."

With some ostentation he dipped his pen in an inkwell and began scribbling in the big ledger.

The boy stood there for a moment, uncertain what to do, then went slowly out the door and down the stairs. This was a blow to his plans that he hadn't counted on. He would have to find a room somewhere and wait until the next day.

Lugging the heavy portmanteau he trudged northward

along Broadway for a block or two, then turned to his right on a side street. The houses here were older and less pretentious. In the window of one of them he saw a card announcing "Board and Room by Day or Week."

A slatternly-looking landlady answered his knock, looked him over and finally accepted him as a tenant. "Third floor, back," she told him. "Half a dollar with breakfast. Lemme see yer money."

He paid her, stowed his bag in the dingy little bedroom and came out into the morning sunshine again. The delay of a day wouldn't be so bad, he thought. Now he had a chance to see the sights of New York.

# *FOUR*

JONATHAN STROLLED SLOWLY DOWN BROADWAY WITH HIS hands in his pockets. It was a fine May day, warm and sunny. He stopped often to stare at new things. Only once or twice in his life had he seen a Negro. There seemed to be a lot of them in the city. Some were slaves, owned by visiting planters from the South. Others—freedmen—worked as stevedores and porters on the docks or drove the high-stepping horses that drew shiny carriages along Broadway.

At St. Paul's Church he turned down to the right toward the North River. Here were more docks, more forests of tall masts. He could see why New York was a great port. It had deep water right up to its streets, besides a broad water highway into the interior and a bay where all the world's ships could drop anchor.

The Hudson River was even more impressive than the Kennebec, he had to admit. The Jersey shore looked far away. To the northward it rose in majestic bluffs, crowned with woods. As he watched, a tiny ferryboat, like a dark waterbug, came puffing out from the opposite bank, steering crab-fashion across the current. Yes, it was a big river.

Fascinated, he followed the waterfront south to the Battery. For an hour or more he stayed there, looking out at the broad reach of the bay—the islands, the ships and the wheeling, screaming gulls.

The ringing of bells for noon reminded him that he had eaten an early breakfast and was hungry again. Along the side streets he had seen several small eating places advertising "Oysters in All Styles." Up in the Kennebec country clams and lobsters and codfish and salmon were common fare, but he had tasted oysters only once or twice in his life.

With a feeling of recklessness he went boldly in the open door of one of these places. The floor was covered deep with sawdust and there were high stools along a bar at one side.

"Wot'll it be, young man?" asked the waiter, wiping the counter with his apron.

"Oysters," said Jonathan.

The man gave him a queer look.

"Yeah," he said. "Wot kind? Half-shell, fried, stewed, broiled, scalloped—say wotcher want."

"I don't know," the boy answered in some confusion. "Whatever way you think is good."

"Dozen raws an' a small stew!" bawled the waiter over his shoulder. He set a bowl of crackers and a glass of water in front of Jonathan and moved away. At the other end of the counter a man in a long white apron was opening oysters. His short, sharp knife moved with lightning speed, and every few seconds a big, gnarled shell clattered on the heap at his feet.

In less than a minute the waiter brought a platter with twelve huge oysters on the half shell. Jonathan looked around for a fork.

"Look," said the waiter. "Like this." He seized one of the boy's oysters, tilted the shell above his upturned mouth and swallowed the bivalve at one convulsive gulp.

Jonathan shivered at the sight but decided to try it. To his surprise, the oyster tasted delicious. He went on and finished the dozen, then ate a bowlful of buttery stew.

"That'll be two bits," said the waiter. "Twenty-fi' cents."

The boy did not argue, though it sounded to him like a

high price. A whole dinner, with roast beef, potatoes, pie and all the fixings, cost only a quarter at the Hallowell House, back home. Still, he had satisfied his curiosity about oysters, and after all, this visit to the metropolis was just once in a lifetime. He jingled the change remaining in his pocket and went out to continue his sightseeing.

All afternoon he wandered through the town, sniffing the pungent smells of pepper, coffee, clove and cinnamon coming from the open doors of warehouses, and the scent of tar from the ship-chandlers' shops. He watched fights between draymen and ran with the crowd that followed the hand-drawn pumpers racing to a fire.

By evening he had had his fill of excitement and his feet were tired with all the tramping he had done on stony pavements. He turned off the Bowery on a dark, narrow street that seemed to lead in the direction of his boarding-house.

It was an unpleasant neighborhood. Dimly lighted taverns, reeking of cheap liquor, stood at the corners of dark alleys. In the tall, rickety houses, families of poor folk were crowded together like animals. He could hear screams and drunken, quarrelsome voices and the squalling of babies as he hurried along. A lean, black alley cat looked at him with baleful yellow eyes and sneaked off into an areaway.

He could see the lights of a more prosperous street a little distance ahead and quickened his pace. There was a sound of padding feet close behind. Uneasy, he looked back and thought he saw a shadow moving in the darkness. His heart was pounding as he hurried on. Then, before he had taken a dozen steps, he heard a scurrying rush and whirled in his tracks. In the gloom all he could see was a ragged figure close upon him. Its upraised arm brandished some kind of club and instinctively Jonathan reached up to seize it. Farm work had given him strong hands. He clutched the man's wrist with a grip of desperation and wrenched it sidewise. His adversary's fingers relaxed their grip and a piece of iron pipe clattered on the pavement.

But the man was wiry and quick. He tried to trip Jonathan, and, when that failed, grappled for his throat with his free hand.

"Help!" yelled the boy at the top of his lungs. "Help! Thieves!"

He drove his right fist at the other's face, but the man ducked. For a moment they struggled, gasping, neither able to gain the advantage. Then there came a pounding of feet from the direction of the lighted street. Jonathan's attacker twisted loose and fled, dodging into a dark alley.

"What's up here?" asked a voice at the boy's elbow. He turned to see a tall man standing there.

"What's up?" the newcomer repeated. "You the lad that hollered for help?"

"Yes, sir," panted Jonathan. "Somebody followed me—tried to knock my brains out with this!"

He stooped and picked up the length of pipe.

"Hm," said the tall man, taking the implement and testing its weight. "A right pretty club! Come on, let's get out o' here. It's a bad part o' town."

He led the way briskly to the corner. Under the gas-light Jonathan could get a better look at him. He was over six feet but slender in build—a man of about thirty, the boy judged. He wore his clothes with an air. His bottle-green coat was shiny and a trifle threadbare, but elegantly cut. Fine doeskin trousers clung tightly to his long legs, their bottoms caught by loops under the insteps of polished boots. His hat was out of key with the rest of his costume. Instead of a stylish tall beaver, he wore a low-crowned black felt hat with a broad brim, tilted at a rakish angle.

"Sort o' shook you up a bit, Bub?" asked the man. He had a queer sort of grin, twisted by a scar at the left corner of his mouth. His eyes were pale gray and glinted sharply in the shadow of the drooping hat brim.

"How about it—he didn't hurt you, did he? Didn't get your money?"

Unconsciously Jonathan's hand moved to his waist, patting the hidden money belt. "No," he said. "I've still got it all safe. And no bones broken."

The tall fellow laughed. "From the way you talk," he said, "I reckon you're a down-east Yankee. My folks used to live in Maine, too. Had your supper yet?"

Jonathan shook his head. "I was going to look for a place to eat," he answered.

"Well, fine," said his new acquaintance heartily. "Come on with me, and we'll pick up a bite together."

Entering a little chop-house in the middle of the next block, they took seats at a corner table. The air was smoky and heavy but fragrant of sputtering steaks and browning roasts. Jonathan's mouth began to water.

"Bring us a couple o' good thick sirloins, on the rare side," the green-coated man told the elderly waiter. "Fried potatoes and all that goes with 'em."

He talked in friendly fashion while they ate. His people on his mother's side were Joneses from Portland, he said. He didn't suppose Jonathan knew the family? Well, that was no matter. They shared the same good Yankee blood. His own name was McKee—Pennsylvania name. Generally known as "Rusty" McKee. He took off his hat with a grin and showed a mop of red hair.

Jonathan gave his own name and explained how he came to be traveling west.

Mr. McKee was interested. "Know all that country well," he nodded. "Been up an' down the Ohio half a dozen times. You'll like Illinois. It's a lot easier to grow crops than back in Maine."

They finished the meal with pie and coffee and the tall man insisted on paying the check. "Glad to have had your company, Brent," he said. "Where are you stoppin'?"

Jonathan told him the street and number. "It's just a few doors from Broadway," he said.

"That's right," Mr. McKee nodded. "Not far from here, either. I'll show you a short cut."

They walked a block or two along the lighted street, and came to a narrow alley.

"Right through here, and we'll come out next door to your boardin'-house," said Jonathan's guide. "You needn't worry about robbers. I'll be right behind you."

The boy turned the corner into the alley. In the darkness he stumbled once or twice over loose stones and groped his way along, touching the brick wall of the building on his right. It was reassuring to have a companion in such a place. McKee was whistling cheerfully, a step behind.

Suddenly the whistle ceased. Something crashed down on the back of Jonathan's head and his senses left him in one flash of blazing, blinding light.

. . .

The first thing he was conscious of was a familiar sound. A rooster crowed somewhere close by. The challenging call was answered from farther away, and in the distance others took it up.

"Morning?" he thought dully. But where was he? What had given him such a splitting headache? He moved a hand and it came in contact with cold, gritty stone. Then he began to remember. He sat up dizzily and blinked his eyes. The dark walls of the buildings rose close on either side, but overhead the sky was paling into dawn. He put his hand to the back of his head and felt a huge lump under the matted hair and dried blood.

With a shock of fear he grabbed at his waist. His jacket was unbuttoned and his shirt open. The money belt was gone! Weakly he slumped back on the dirty pavement, overcome by a wave of misery and self-reproach.

How could he have let himself be taken in so easily by McKee? Bitterly he vowed that he would never trust a stranger again. That was little help, except that in his rage at his own gullibility he forgot his aching head.

Jonathan got to his hands and knees and managed to stagger to his feet. For a moment he leaned against the wall till his legs felt strong enough to walk. With fumbling fingers he pulled his shirt together and buttoned his jacket. Feeling in his pocket he found forty cents in change and his jackknife. The letter to Jeremiah Parsons was no longer there.

He looked around him dully and caught sight of a piece of paper in the mud of the alley. When he picked it up and smoothed its rumpled surface he could see the blurred salutation—"Jeremiah Parsons, Esq." But the following message was so smeared with mud that he could hardly read a word of it. Wiping it off as best he could, he put the letter back in his pocket and started slowly toward the street at the end of the alley.

The time, he thought, must be about five o'clock in the morning. The daylight came slowly through an overcast sky. He carried his muddy cap in his hand, for the lump on his head was still painful. When he reached Broadway he sat down on a step and tried to think.

The loss of the money was the thing that weighed most on his spirits. He knew he must continue his journey, for his father needed him. But first he ought to report the robbery to the authorities. It might be possible to recover the $500 that had been in the buckskin bag, sewn to his money-belt.

Early morning traffic was beginning to rattle over the pavement. A milk-cart came by, the driver banging his dipper against one of the big copper cans. "Getcher milk!" he bawled. "Getcher fresh mi-i-ilk!"

An aproned serving-maid, with a crock in her hands, came hurrying down the steps of a near-by house and a quart of milk was ladled out for her.

As the milkman went on down the street, Jonathan saw a police constable strolling toward him along the sidewalk. The officer stopped in front of a shop window to admire his reflection. He flicked a speck of dust off the sleeve of his jacket, brushed the flowing ends of his big mustache, and moved nearer, twirling his billy by its strap.

Jonathan got up. He was still dizzy and had to hold on to

the iron railing beside the steps. As he started to speak, the constable caught sight of him and scowled.

"Move along now," he ordered, lifting his stick threateningly. "We want no vagrants around here."

"But," the boy faltered, "I—I just wanted to tell you—I've been robbed."

The officer leered. "A likely story, me lad!" he said, casting a supercilious eye over Jonathan's rumpled hair and muddy clothes. "Robbed o' what—a penny?"

"Five hundred dollars," the boy told him. "I had it here in my belt. A man who called himself McKee hit me on the head and stole it."

"Ho, ho, ho!" The constable tipped his head back and roared. "A young rascal like you with five hundred dollars! That's a good un."

His scowl returned. "Take yerself out o' here, an' let's hear no more cock-an'-bull tales!" he growled.

"But it's true," gasped Jonathan. "I was traveling west from Maine—taking the money to my father. I—"

The policeman raised his club again and looked as if he meant to use it. Seeing the hopelessness of argument, Jonathan moved slowly away, down the street. He clenched his teeth, blinking to keep the tears back. It was the first time in his experience that anyone had ever doubted his word.

"All right," he told himself fiercely, "I'll make it somehow. I'll get to Illinois, money or no money."

# FIVE

THE SIDE STREET WHERE HE HAD RENTED A ROOM WAS JUST ahead, and Jonathan stumbled along it till he came to the house. At his second or third knock, the landlady appeared in a wrapper and curl-papers. She failed to recognize him at first and was about to slam the door in his face. When he finally convinced her that he was the same young man who had taken the room she looked him over sharply.

"Been out roisterin' around all night, I see," she snapped. "You can just take your luggage an' get out o' here. I want no rakes an' brawlers. This is a respectable place."

He tried to explain what had happened to him, though she obviously believed very little of his story. At last she allowed him to come inside and served him a grudging breakfast of bread and tea.

There was a cracked washbowl and pitcher in his room, and there he washed as best he could and combed his hair. Vigorous brushing removed most of the dried mud from his clothes and he changed to a clean shirt. When he finished he looked almost respectable once more.

He took his bag and departed without a farewell. Fortunately his legs felt steadier now, and the throbbing in his head was less intense. It was a little after eight when he climbed the stairs to the Parsons counting-house.

The same clerk who had talked to him the day before looked up and frowned when he came in.

"No," he said, "Mr. Parsons ain't been in. An' from what I hear he's likely to be away the rest o' the week—up to Albany on business, he is."

Jonathan pulled the letter out of his pocket, looked at its hopelessly soiled and blotted writing and put it back. Leaving it for Parsons would be worse than useless, for the merchant couldn't possibly read it.

He thanked the clerk for his information and lugged the portmanteau down to the street again.

It was the shrill toot of a ferryboat whistle on the East River that made him think of the *Phoebe Foster*. There were Maine men aboard her—folks who would believe what he told them and help him if they could.

But where was the schooner now? Captain Foster had expected to sail last night if all went well, but something might have delayed him. With a desperate hope that he would find the little ship still at the wharf, he started running toward the waterfront.

The clumsy bag got in his way, and twice he stumbled and nearly fell. He was panting hard when he reached the dockside. Brushing the sweat out of his eyes, he peered at the spot where the schooner had been moored, and his heart fell. It was empty.

A big Irish stevedore was standing close by. "What's the trouble wid ye, lad?" he asked the forlorn youngster.

"There was a two-master here yesterday," Jonathan told him. "The *Phoebe Foster,* out of Gardiner. I guess she sailed."

"Right," nodded the Irishman. "But not far. I kin see the masts av her this minute, yonder on the Brooklyn side. She was to take a bit more cargo an' leave, the morn."

"How can I get over there before she sails?" gasped Jonathan.

"Ye could take the ferry," the man replied, scratching his chin. "But ye'd have a long walk. There's a bit av a boat below here ye might borry."

"Where?" asked the boy. "You mean it belongs to some

friend of yours?"

The Irishman winked solemnly. "Not as ye might say a close friend," he replied. " 'Tis the dockmaster's boat. But he won't be missin' it—not before noon."

He led the way down some rickety wooden stairs and pointed to an old skiff, moored to the piling.

"In wid ye," he said. "Can ye row?"

Jonathan tossed his bag into the bottom of the boat, untied the painter and seized the oars. "Yes," he said. "And thank you. I'll leave it on the other side, at that pier where the schooner is."

He swung the bow out into the river and began pulling on the oars. It was farther than he had thought, and a tide was running, sweeping the little boat to the right, in the direction of the bay. He had to put extra power on the left-hand oar. Once a steamboat churned by, its paddles tossing up a heavy wake that made the skiff bounce like a cork.

Jonathan didn't stop rowing till he was almost under the schooner's counter. He pulled in under the wharf and made fast the painter with fumbling fingers. Then he pushed the skiff's stern around and managed to reach a barnacle-encrusted ladder, nailed to the side of the dock. Somehow he got himself and his portmanteau up to the solid planking.

The last barrel was being rolled aboard the *Phoebe Foster.*

"Stand by to cast off!" bellowed the familiar voice of the

skipper.

Jonathan didn't wait on ceremony. He jumped hastily across to the deck, landing among the startled crew.

Captain Foster whirled and stared at him open-mouthed. "What we got here?" he cried. "Jonathan Brent, by the great horned spoon! What's up, lad?"

Wearily the boy panted out his story—Parsons' absence—his struggle with the footpad and the timely aid of the man in the green coat—the sudden blow on the head and the loss of his money.

"The police wouldn't listen to me," he finished. "And Mr. Parsons won't be back for a week. I figured maybe you'd let me ship as a sailor to Baltimore, an' I could go on west from there."

The captain's jaw jutted grimly. " 'Pears they didn't treat ye so good ashore," he said. "Bend over here an' let's look at that head."

His blunt fingers explored the wound gently. "Broke the scalp," he announced, "but I reckon he didn't bust yer skull. I b'lieve I've got some stickin'-plaster in my locker, an' I'll patch ye up. After that we'll go over an' talk to the law-officers. Won't sail till next tide."

Two of the *Phoebe Foster's* crew rowed them across the river, towing the "borrowed" skiff, which Jonathan tied up where he had found it. From the wharf, he accompanied the captain up the hill to the bleak stone building known as the "Tombs." It was inside this forbidding structure that the city watch made its headquarters.

Captain Foster got a civil reception from the guard at the gate and they were shown into a bare, poorly lighted room where the officer in charge greeted them. The skipper stated the facts briefly and Jonathan told the whole story in detail. The policeman took down an accurate description of the man who called himself McKee, and asked several other questions about exact times and places, which Jonathan answered as well as he could.

"We'll have every man in the watch looking out for the fellow," the officer assured them. "Might pick him up tonight. Might be a week or two."

The captain thanked him. "I'm sailin' for Baltimore this evenin'," he explained. "An' the boy's goin' along with me. I'll put in at New York again in ten days an' see what ye've found."

When they were outside again Captain Foster blew a loud blast into his bandanna handkerchief. "Don't like the graveyard smell o' that place," he said. "No wonder they call it the Tombs. I wouldn't put too much faith in their gittin' yer money back, son, but I'll stop in an' remind 'em on the home v'yage."

As they walked back to the waterfront, Jonathan brought up the matter of the trip to Baltimore again. "I don't want you to take me as a passenger," he said. "If you could ship me before the mast I'd try an' earn my keep. All I've got left is forty cents."

The leathery lines crinkled at the corners of the captain's eyes, but he replied with proper gravity. "No doubt at all ye'll make a prime hand," he said. "We ain't exactly short of able seamen on the *Phoebe Foster,* but I reckon we can use one more—for two-three days, anyhow. I'll sign ye on proper an' pay ye the reg'lar lay."

Back aboard the schooner again, Jonathan began to feel better. The crew grinned when he put his bag in a bunk in the forecastle, but they gave him a hearty welcome. Two or three of them were Kennebec farm boys like himself and not much older. Instead of treating him with the contempt he might have expected as a landlubber, they set about teaching him the ropes.

He learned fast. All afternoon the schooner lay at anchor out in the river, saving dock fees while she waited for the tide. By sunset the boy knew the name and purpose of every halliard and stay. He jumped to the capstan when the skipper gave orders to weigh anchor, and he walked it round with a will. With any encouragement he would gladly have taken his trick at the wheel.

They moved slowly down past Castle Garden and into the bay on the ebbing tide. Once clear of the tip of Manhattan they picked up a little wind from the west and were well down through the Narrows before darkness fell. The red and green running lights were lit. It was a clear night and good sailing.

Jonathan had been assigned to the watch that was on deck until midnight, and he spent his time forward with the bow lookout. The sailor was a big, brawny youngster from Damariscotta, who talked with a down-east twang and had been around boats from the time he could walk. In spite of the fact that he was only eighteen, he knew the coast all the way south to the Bahamas—every light and shoal and headland—as well as he knew the river back home.

"That's Sandy Hook to sta'board," he told Jonathan. "Beyond's the Jersey Highlands. An' after that, nothin' but flat sand beach. It's a mean shore in a northeast gale, but fine in this kind o' weather. No reefs. How d'ye aim to travel after ye git to Baltimore?"

"I'll have to figure as I go along," said Jonathan. "They say there's a steam railroad up from Baltimore to a place called York, in Pennsylvania. That's on the big wagon road west across the mountains. An' there's a canal, too, that could take me to Pittsburgh. From there it ought to be easy to get down the Ohio on some sort o' boat. I won't have any money but I can work my way along, I reckon."

"Gee!" The sailor sighed. "Takes plenty o' spunk to tackle a trip like that. I never been any place much—except in ships—to Liverpool an' Lisbon an' Caracas an' such ports."

He said it with complete seriousness. A thousand-mile journey overland seemed to him a staggering undertaking, and his envy and admiration were real. Jonathan grinned a little in the darkness.

The schooner made a fine long reach of it down the Jersey coast. A west wind blew briskly, filling the close-hauled sails. Just before they went below, at midnight, the lookout pointed to a pin-point of light low over the starboard bow. "Know what that is?" he asked.

"Maybe a star just setting?" Jonathan suggested.

"Nope. That's Barnegat Light. When we pull abreast of it we'll be halfway down to the Delaware Capes. Must be loggin' 'round eight knots."

By the light of the big forecastle lantern, Jonathan took off his boots and jacket and tumbled into his bunk. The ache was gone from his head but he was very tired. Half a minute after he turned in he was asleep.

His watch was called at four in the morning, but the good-hearted crew didn't disturb the boy's slumbers. He was somewhat crestfallen to find it broad day when he finally woke.

They were close enough inshore to see half-wild cattle feeding on the dunes of Seven-Mile Beach that morning. Before noon the schooner was off Cape May and sailing past the mouth of Delaware Bay. Then a shift of wind to the southwest slowed their progress. For the rest of the day, they were forced to beat to windward along the Delaware and Maryland coast. The hands on deck were kept busy hauling the sheets and ducking the booms as the craft came about, and Jonathan learned more seamanship. He took his regular watch that night. It was two bells in the morning watch when the skipper ordered the schooner hove to.

"Fog's gettin' thick," he said, "an' this breeze is due to die. We're off Cape Charles now. If the weather lifts by daylight, we can sail into the Roads."

Through the shrouding mist they could hear distant fog bells and the occasional wail of a whistle. Other ships were anchored like themselves. It was not until late in the forenoon that a fresh breeze stirred the fog and they could see where they were.

Captain Foster studied the low-lying coast when it became visible. "That'll be Cape Charles, right enough," he announced. "Get that anchor up an' make sail."

They entered Hampton Roads under a cloudy sky. A full-rigged ship was less than a mile ahead of them, beating south toward Norfolk, and other craft of all sizes were in sight. A few miles inside the Capes, Jonathan was thrilled to see a fifty-gun U. S. frigate on patrol.

The southwest breeze favored them all the way up the Chesapeake, and they were off the mouth of the Potomac when night fell. Again there were signs of fog. The schooner dropped anchor to wait for daylight and clearer skies, and

Jonathan got another good night's rest.

It was late afternoon of the following day when the *Phoebe Foster* made her way up the Patapsco River to Baltimore. The waterfront was lined with shipping—tall masts and spars and a network of cordage against the sunset sky. This was a great port, as Jonathan could see. A great town and an old town, with a solid respectability about it that even New York had lacked.

When the schooner was safely berthed, Captain Foster clapped his apprentice seaman on the back. "Come on ashore with me, son," he grinned. "We'll find out about them railroad trains, an' maybe git a bite to eat. They have their own kind o' vittles here, an' not bad-tastin' either. Crabs are sort of a specialty. Terrapin's another. Oysters, too, if ye like 'em."

They climbed through narrow streets, lined with ship-chandlers' shops, and found the railway station. A steam engine on wheels—the first one Jonathan had seen—was puffing and belching clouds of smoke on one of the tracks. With its long black boiler and huge wood-burner stack it looked enormous to the boy, and he was amazed at the ease with which it moved two or three box-like freight cars along the rails. The captain fairly had to pull him away.

The train to York, they were told, would leave at eight-thirty in the morning. Jonathan saw some money pass between the skipper and the man behind the desk. Then Captain Foster put a piece of pasteboard in his hand.

"That there's yer ticket, boy," he said. "Give it to the conductor feller when he asks for it on the train. No—keep that change in yer pocket. This here's out o' yer pay."

They dined on oysters, deviled crab and terrapin stew and went back to sleep aboard the schooner. Before Jonathan went to the forecastle, the captain asked him down to the cabin.

"Near as I can figger it, I owe ye a couple o' dollars for the v'yage," he said, and handed him two bills, folded together. "Put that in yer safest pocket an' keep out o' dark alleys," he chuckled. "It won't let ye travel in much style, but at least it'll buy a meal or two."

Jonathan knew well that he hadn't earned two dollars, let alone the cost of his railroad ticket. He started to say as much, but realized it would embarrass the good skipper. Instead, he thanked him, pocketed the money and went forward to his bunk.

It wasn't until two days later and a hundred miles away that he looked at the folded notes again. Only then did he discover that the inner one was a twenty-dollar bill.

# SIX

THE WEATHER SMILED ON JONATHAN'S START. IT WAS ONE OF those summery May mornings that are nowhere lovelier than in Maryland. As the boy carried his portmanteau toward the station, he saw dozens of Negro servants scrubbing the white marble steps of narrow red brick houses. Their rich, drawling voices and bubbling laughter were full of the same lazy sunshine that bathed the street. They were, he supposed, slaves, for he was in slave territory now. But surely no human beings he had ever seen were more contented with their lot. Coming from Maine, where the rumblings of the abolitionists were already beginning to be heard, he was puzzled. It seemed that not all slaves were ill-treated.

At the railroad station he found the train already made up and waiting. The passenger coaches almost took his breath away. Instead of the converted stage-coach bodies he had seen in pictures, these were handsomely painted affairs, each at least twenty feet long, and with a row of glass windows in the side. There was a roofed-over platform with steps at the front and rear of each car, and they were fastened together with heavy iron chains.

The fireman was throwing chunks of cordwood into a fire-box under the boiler. Just behind the engine was a small, flat-topped car piled high with birch and pine fuel. It was still twenty minutes before the time of departure, but a roaring fire was needed to get steam up.

Seeing other passengers going aboard, Jonathan climbed the steps and entered one of the cars. Aside from the stains of tobacco juice on the floor it was the most luxurious conveyance he had ever seen. It fairly glittered with brass fittings. There were two oil lamps in ornate brass hangers overhead. The upholstered seats were bound with the same metal. And there were brass spittoons at strategic points along the aisle.

With a feeling of awe at all this magnificence, the boy removed his cap, put down his bag and sat gingerly on one of the seats. It was less comfortable than it looked, for the springs were very firm under the plush, but he felt like a millionaire as he leaned back and surveyed the scene. The car filled up gradually. There were tearful good-byes on the platform. Ladies who had not traveled by steam before asked excitedly for their smelling-salts, and told their husbands they were sure to faint at such high speeds. Babies cried, dogs barked, the engine blew a loud shriek on its whistle, the conductor shouted "All aboard!"—and at last, with a great puffing and jerking, the train got under way.

Jonathan hung onto the edge of his seat, but for the first mile he was a little disappointed. The engine crept along through city streets at a pace hardly faster than a man could walk. Its bell kept up a tremendous din, warning carriages and pedestrians at the crossings. Occasionally a horse would snort and rear at sight of the passing monster.

Then at last they were out in the country and the rails clicked more rapidly under the iron-shod wheels. A cloud of black smoke and sparks swept back past the window. Looking out he could see trees and houses rushing by at a frightening rate. One of the nervous ladies let out a squeal and was reassured by her husband who sounded none too calm himself.

The conductor came through, bracing his legs wide against the jolting of the coach, and collecting the tickets as he went along.

"Conductor," asked a tremulous female voice just behind Jonathan, "conductor, how fast are we going?"

"Well, ma'am," he replied heartily, "we ain't quite at top speed yet, but I'd calc'late about twenty-five miles an hour."

There was a chorus of exclamations at this news. Twenty-five miles an hour! Astounding! They were living in an age of speed indeed!

Up ahead on the highway that paralleled the track, Jonathan could see a chaise behind a pair of fast trotters. The driver heard the engine and leaned forward, flourishing his whip, and the horses' legs flashed in quickened rhythm. He could see they were doing their best, but it wasn't good enough. Little by little the train gained on them, then passed them. The last glimpse Jonathan had of the team made him sorrowful, for he liked good horses. Far back along the road they were plunging crazily, forced beyond their gait by the whip. That settled it. He would never again doubt the power of steam.

The train clattered through a pleasant countryside of farms, stopped at one or two villages and entered a barren stretch of scrub pine woods. Several times it ground to a jerky halt beside wood piles, where the fuel on the tender was replenished.

The journey had lasted about three hours, and they were already over the state line in Pennsylvania, when there came a frenzied toot of the whistle and a squeal of brakes. The lady passengers set up an outcry and clutched the seats as a sudden bump shook the car. Then the train jolted to a stop and everybody made a dash for the doors.

When Jonathan got outside he saw a huddle of passengers gathering around the locomotive. The engineer and fireman were on their hands and knees by the pilot wheels, trying to pull something out from under the engine. The boy shoved through the crowd till he had a closer view. Wedged under the wheels was the battered carcass of a huge hog.

There was much loud talk and helpful advice from the male passengers, but all the crew's efforts to remove the dead porker were in vain. After the better part of an hour the farmer who owned the hog arrived. He was a burly, slow-spoken Pennsylvania Dutchman, and when he saw his mangled property he was very angry. The hog, it appeared, was a most superior animal, far more valuable than the run of the breed. Its owner said it was worth fifteen dollars and demanded payment on the spot.

At last the conductor succeeded in explaining that a claim would have to be sent to the railroad—that it was against the rules for the crew to give him any money out of their own pockets. Still grumbling and swearing in his guttural

German dialect, the farmer stumped off. He returned presently with a team of big work horses and a chain, and in two or three minutes he had pulled the carcass out.

The accident seemed to have caused some damage to the engine. At any rate the train made very slow time on the last ten miles of its run, and limped into York more than two hours late.

Jonathan felt a twinge of homesickness as he stood on the station platform with his bulky bag. All around him there was a hubbub of greetings—ladies kissing each other—passengers recounting the terrors of the trip—relatives asking about Uncle Joseph and Aunt Samantha.

The Harrisburg mail coach had been held until the arrival of the train, and now the driver began urging people to get aboard if they wanted to reach the state capital before midnight. The vehicle was already bulging with passengers and there were half a dozen sitting on top when Jonathan reached it. He asked about the fare and was told it would cost him four dollars and he'd better hustle if he meant to go. After a moment's indecision he made up his mind that he wouldn't spend any such sum to travel a mere thirty miles.

The driver cracked his long-lashed whip, the horses plunged into their collars, and the coach went off in a whirl of dust. Left alone on the platform, the boy shouldered his bag and started walking westward through the town.

The hot sunshine poured down on him and he soon shed his coat. In half an hour he was out of the town itself and striding along a highway through green fields. This was fine farming country. He wished Uncle Eli could be there to see the great red barns, the well-cultivated corn, and the green fields of tobacco.

Several times he was passed by private carriages or farm wagons, but nobody offered him a lift. By four o'clock he was both hungry and thirsty, and his portmanteau seemed to weigh more with every step. He turned in at the next dooryard. The neat, white farmhouse stood in the shade of a pair of big chestnut trees, and there was a well with a tall sweep close to the front step.

Jonathan set down his bag, wiped his dripping face and knocked at the door. A plump, stolid-faced Dutch girl opened it and stood there staring at him.

He took off his cap. " 'Afternoon, ma'am," he said. "Do you mind if I get a drink at the well?"

She smiled then and came out, nodding. Before he could do it for himself she had lifted the weighted end of the sweep, plunging the bucket down into the well. It came up again, dripping, and the boy drank eagerly. The water was cold and clear and delicious.

"Gee!" he breathed. "That's good!"

"Ya," the girl laughed. "Goot–goot!"

She asked a question in such broken English that he

couldn't understand, then ran into the house. In a moment she came out again with half a loaf of crusty white bread, a big wedge of cheese and a pitcher of buttermilk.

Jonathan took a quarter from his pocket and tried to pay her, but she refused with many gestures and smiles. Finally, seeing that she meant it, he thanked her, sat down on the well curb and enjoyed his simple repast. His appetite wasn't spoiled by the fact that the good-hearted girl stood there watching every mouthful he ate.

A little breeze had sprung up and it was cooler when he started on. He must have made another five or six miles that evening before dusk fell. By that time he had come to the conclusion that his portmanteau was a mistake. His arms ached, and his legs were bruised from the bumping of the heavy bag.

When it began to grow dark he stopped to drink at a small brook in a grove of trees by the road. Just beyond he saw the remnants of a straw stack, standing by itself in a field. Burrowing into the side of it he soon made himself a comfortable nest. He crawled in, pillowed his head on his rolled-up jacket, and lay there listening to the rustle of the straw in the evening breeze. Field mice squeaked and scampered and insects chirped around him. In a minute or two he drowsed off to sleep.

Just before sunrise some bits of chaff fell on his face and tickled him awake. He rubbed his cheek and looked up to see the small bright eyes of a song sparrow peering down at him. At his movement the bird flew away and he pulled himself out of his bed.

Another fine day was beginning. He stretched his arms and listened to the chorus of birdsong coming from the near-by grove. When he had washed in the brook and had another drink of water in lieu of breakfast, he felt ready for anything. Even the portmanteau seemed to be lighter.

He had walked only half a mile along the road when a farm wagon came out of a lane just ahead of him. The driver pulled his team to a stop and waited till Jonathan came up. He looked the boy up and down with a quizzical grin.

"Come fur, young feller?" he asked.

"State of Maine," replied Jonathan.

"Hm," said the farmer, considering this information. "Goin' fur?" he asked.

"Illinois," the boy told him with a straight face.

"Hm. Well, if Harrisburg's on yer way I can carry ye a piece. Hop up here."

Jonathan needed no second invitation. He climbed over the wheel and when he was settled on the plank seat, the man clucked to his horses.

"Don't generally pick anybody up," he remarked. "Too many rogues an' rascals on the roads these days. But I took a good look at ye. Seen ye was jest a young shaver, an' totin' a heavy bag. Come from Maine, ye say?"

"That's right. Sailed as far as Baltimore in a Kennebec schooner, an' took the railroad to York."

He answered some more of the farmer's questions about Maine, and asked a few of his own. There were two packet lines running daily trips out of Harrisburg on the canal, he learned—the "Express" and the "Pioneer" lines.

"Ain't much to choose," the Pennsylvanian told him. "They say the Express boats give ye more room to sleep, but the Pioneers gen'ly git thar faster. Both of 'em rob ye. Forty dollars to Pittsburgh they want, countin' the meals."

This news was a blow to Jonathan's plans. He thought about the sum of money in his pocket and wondered what other means of transport he could find.

"How fast do the freight wagons make it over the mountains?" he asked.

"Dunno. Mebbe two weeks," said the farmer. "Mebbe more."

"And the packet boats?"

"Oh, they step right along. Only takes 'em 'bout four days. If ye're strapped fer money, ye might try fer a job drivin' or workin' as a deckhand. I've heered o' travelers doin' that."

After a while the road led down a hill toward a broad, slow-flowing river. It was a shallow-looking stream, with rocks and riffles blocking its channel. But its banks were lined with trees now in full leaf, and it had a peaceful beauty quite different from the majesty of the Kennebec.

"What river is that?" the boy asked.

The farmer looked at him, surprised. "Why," he said, "I thought ever'body in the world knew the Susquehanna. Mebbe ye wouldn't, though, bein' from way off there in Maine."

There were little green islands dotted over the river's expanse, and occasionally Jonathan saw a fisherman drowsing in his boat. There was a golden morning light over the valley. The scene made the boy think of those handsome landscapes he had seen in the colored prints published by Mr. Currier of New York.

After two hours or more of driving along the river's shore, they sighted a long, covered bridge in the distance.

"That's the bridge acrost to Harrisburg," the farmer explained. "Reckon it's the biggest in the world—leastways 'round these parts. Pretty nigh a mile from end to end."

Jonathan had seen plenty of covered bridges but he was ready to believe the man's statement about this one. Certainly it was the longest he had ever crossed. After the bright sunshine the gloom inside its wooden roof and walls was like night, and the opening at the opposite end was no more than a pin-point of light. The hoof-beats of the horses and the rumble of the wheels reverberated like thunder.

"Well," said the farmer, when they emerged at last on

the farther shore, "this here's the town o' Harrisburg. I'm goin' this way, down to Belcher's feed store. The canal's up yonder. Never mind thankin' me, son. Glad to have yer comp'ny. Hope ye git to Illinois safe 'n' sound."

And with those friendly words he swung the team south, leaving the grateful boy standing by the roadside.

# SEVEN

IT WAS NOW NEAR NOON, AND JONATHAN HAD BEEN AWARE for some time of a very empty stomach. He walked along the streets of the bustling little state capital and eventually found a modest eating place. For thirty cents he had a big plate of roast beef and potatoes, bread and butter, pickles and preserves, pie and something that passed as coffee.

With food under his belt he tackled his next job, which was to locate the canal and see what he could do about getting transportation west. A few inquiries and a walk of half a dozen blocks brought him to the canal basin.

There were big wooden signs advertising the rival packet lines, and under each a boat lay moored. These canal packets were a new type of craft to Jonathan. They sat low in the water—long, squat barges with cabins occupying most of their length. No passengers had yet gone aboard, for the boats always waited for the afternoon train to come in from Philadelphia. That much the boy learned from a teamster who was feeding his horses on the canal bank.

"Do you drive on the canal?" Jonathan asked him.

"Yep. Red Lion freighters," the man replied, shooting an amber stream of tobacco juice into the placid water. "Takin' out that boat yonder in 'bout an hour."

He pointed to a deep-laden boat tied up among a dozen others beyond the packet landing. The freighters had long cargo holds, with tiny cabins aft and stables forward.

"I don't suppose you travel as fast as the passenger boats," Jonathan remarked.

"Heck, no! We tie up nights to rest the team. Takes us four days to the mountains—ten days to Pittsburgh."

"Do you ever carry passengers?" the boy asked.

"Nope. Ain't room. Cap'n an' cook fill up the cabin. Us drivers sleep with the hosses. If ye're tryin' to git west why don't ye ask the skipper o' the Pioneer boat. He might make out to use a roustabout. That's him settin' out there on deck."

Jonathan picked up his bag and went across the gangplank to the packet. The individual who had been pointed out to him was a short, very fat man with a fringe of red whiskers surrounding his moon-like face. He wore a nautical-looking cap at a jaunty angle and was smoking a cob pipe. When he saw Jonathan, the stout chair in which he had been leaning back came down on its front legs with a thump.

"Yessir," chirped the captain. "Passenger on the Pioneer? How fur ye travelin'?"

"Er—no," the boy hastened to tell him. "I'm not really a passenger, but I'd sure like to get to Pittsburgh. Could you use a hand?"

The fat man scowled and leaned back again with a sniff. "Seems like they's more dead-beats on the canal than payin' folks," he complained. "No, I got my reg'lar crew. Ye might pick up a dime or a quarter helpin' load baggage when the folks come aboard from the train."

Jonathan had no better luck when he asked about a job on the Express packet. In the vague hope that one of the deckhands might fail to show up, he sat down on his portmanteau to wait.

There was plenty of activity along the canal. Drays clattered up and unloaded boxes and barrels that were stowed in the holds of the freight boats. After a while he saw the Red Lion driver hitching up his team. The boat's skipper took his place at the tiller, blew a long blast on a cow-horn,

THE ENGINE WHISTLED AT THE EDGE OF TOWN

and guided the boat out into the canal as the horses dug in to pull.

From time to time other boats departed or came in to the moorings at the end of their long journey. The arrival of a boat from the west was a cause of considerable stir and excitement. Merchants came down to the canal to look over the freight and ask about shipments they had ordered. The bulk of the east-bound cargoes seemed to be flour and Monongahela whisky, with an occasional bundle of beaver skins or buffalo hides.

The train, expected to arrive at four o'clock, failed to appear. Several passengers had already gone aboard the packets, and as time dragged on they began to fidget and look at their watches.

Six o'clock came, and still no train. The cook on the Pioneer boat set up trestle tables in the long cabin and a smell of hot food was wafted out to Jonathan. Supper was being served.

It was beginning to grow dark when the engine whistled at the edge of town. At once the boat crews bestirred themselves. The three-horse teams were led down from the company stables and hitched up in tandem. Because of the speed they were expected to maintain, these packet horses were lighter and more spirited than the work-nags that pulled the freighters. The packet lines had relay stations every fifteen or twenty miles along the canal, where the teams were changed.

In a few minutes carriages and rigs of various kinds began arriving from the railroad station. Jonathan offered his services in carrying baggage aboard the Pioneer boat and soon had all the work he could handle. The travelers' equipment ranged from battered carpet-bags to heavy trunks and chests.

Only the lighter hand-luggage was taken into the cabin. All the heavier pieces were piled on top of the cabin and a long tarpaulin was thrown over them for protection against the dew and rain. Jonathan labored hard at the job and a number of the passengers gave him tips. He had collected forty-five cents by the time everything was aboard.

The Pioneer driver climbed into the saddle on the lead horse, the fat skipper stood by the tiller, and it appeared that the boat was finally ready to start its trip. Just then there came a great clatter of hoofs and wheels. Above the general hubbub someone shouted, "Whoa! Hold on thar! 'Nother passenger fer the Pioneer!"

Jonathan saw a chaise, pulled by a lathered horse, come rattling down to the dock and stop a few yards from where he stood. A man swung down over the wheel. Even in the half darkness the boy knew him instantly. The doeskin trousers—the broad-brimmed black hat—the scar-twisted mouth. It was his recent acquaintance, "Rusty" McKee!

The tall man flung a piece of paper money to the driver

of the chaise and strode over to the gangplank. And Jonathan, acting on a sudden impulse, picked up his own portmanteau and darted after him. The boy had been on and off the boat a dozen times that evening so nobody paid any attention to him. He put the bag on top of the cabin with the other luggage, and while McKee was aft, talking to the captain, he slipped in under the tarpaulin between two trunks. The dusk and the confusion favored him. In a moment he heard the order given to cast off, and then, slowly but surely, the packet was moving!

. . .

It was some time before the boy was in any condition to think clearly. He lay there in his cramped nest, hardly daring to breathe, listening to footsteps passing close by on the deck. Directly under him, in the cabin, there was a buzz of conversation and a clink of china, as the passengers finished their meal. Then he heard the tables being removed and the berths put in order for the night. The ladies, he knew, slept forward and the men aft, separated by a curtain.

Taking stock of his situation, Jonathan found himself wondering just how he came to be aboard the packet. True, he was anxious to go westward and had thought once or twice of trying to stow away during that long afternoon. But it was the sight of the man who had robbed him that had spurred him to action. Somehow he had to keep close to McKee—watch his movements and, if the chance offered, turn him over to the law.

How he was going to get food and exercise while hiding aboard the boat was more than he knew. Probably the whole idea was crazy. But as long as the tow-team was pulling him west at six miles an hour he refused to worry. He could hear the thud of their trotting feet up ahead on the hard-beaten path.

A hail came back from the driver. "Lo-o-w bridge!" And a deckhand somewhere a few feet away repeated the call. Jonathan got a momentary scare when he heard someone fumbling at the piled baggage and felt the tarpaulin twitch as it was pulled tighter. That was all that happened. One of the crew was merely making sure that the load was low enough to clear the bridge.

After a time the boy drowsed off. In spite of his uncomfortable position he slept until dawn, and was only wakened by the noise of early risers getting out of their berths in the cabin below. He was aching in every bone after lying in one position all night. There was barely room to turn over in the narrow space where he lay, but he managed it somehow. A moment later several of the male passengers came up to stretch their legs. They stood a few feet from his hiding place, coughing, yawning and grumbling about their crowded sleeping quarters.

He was to hear those same voices often during the long day that followed. He came to recognize them and tried to picture what their owners looked like. There was one pompous New Yorker who found this travel through the backwoods most depressing and assured his hearers that he would never stir off Manhattan again. There were drawling Tennesseans and thick-tongued Dutchmen, and later, when the ladies came on deck, he heard the mincing accents of Philadelphia finishing schools.

If he had been less hungry, thirsty and uncomfortable, Jonathan might have found the scraps of talk entertaining. As it was he had to exercise all his will power to keep from groaning aloud as the hours dragged by. The smell of hot food came up to him tantalizingly at noon and again at suppertime and made his empty stomach writhe with hunger.

By the time darkness fell the boy was desperate. His mouth was dry and his lips swollen, for he had tasted no water in thirty hours. He waited until he heard the last passenger toss his cigar butt in the canal and go below. Then he started to crawl painfully out from under the canvas. When he got his feet on the deck he found he was so weak and dizzy he could hardly stand. There was no moon, and in the darkness he couldn't even make out the figure of the steersman.

It was only a yard to the rail. He clutched it and leaned over, hearing the tempting gurgle of water a few feet below. If he had a bucket he thought he could lean down far enough to dip some up. He turned back and fumbled in the dark along the side of the deck house, searching for something—anything—that would hold water.

A light footstep sounded, close behind him. Jonathan crouched in the shadow and held his breath, but a hand gripped his shoulder, jerking him erect.

A lucifer match sputtered and flared and he was looking into the cold, light eyes of "Rusty" McKee.

"Well!" ejaculated the tall man under his breath. "My young friend from Maine, eh? Brent, I think you told me your name was. Hm—stowin' away on a canal packet! That ain't right, you know—liable to get you in trouble."

He turned, as if to call the captain, and Jonathan knew he had to act quickly. Squirming loose from the other's grasp he darted to the rail and flung himself over. The shock of the cold water seemed to revive his strength, and he swam hard for the bank only a few yards away. As he clung to the grass below the tow-path the stern of the boat swished past.

"What the devil was that?" he heard the man at the tiller ask, and there came an answearing peal of laughter from McKee.

"Just a muskrat, I reckon," the scar-faced man chuckled, as the packet pulled swiftly away.

Jonathan choked back tears of rage and weakness. An uncontrollable fit of shivering shook his body. He had to get out of the canal, but first he had to drink. The water was stagnant and probably dirty but to his parched throat it tasted like nectar. He drank slowly and not too much. Then, somewhat revived, he succeeded in hauling himself up the bank.

For a moment he lay there panting, but the night wind blew on his wet body and started him shivering again. He struggled up, threshed his arms and forced himself to run along the tow-path. Somehow—perhaps by instinct—his stumbling feet took him westward. Certainly his mind had little to do with it, for hunger and discouragement threw a haze over his conscious thoughts.

He had no idea how long he had been running when his knees buckled under him and he fell full length on the ground. Lying there, panting, he tried to pull himself together and consider what he should do next.

His portmanteau, with all the clothes he owned except those on his back, was gone. So was his means of transportation, and with it his opportunity to keep McKee in sight.

On the other hand he was still alive and all in one piece. He still had the money Captain Foster had given him. And he was halfway across Pennsylvania, with the Ohio River only a hundred and fifty miles away. If he could find a place where he could get something to eat, perhaps things wouldn't look so black after all.

Somewhere off there in the night, not too far from the canal, was the Conestoga Road. For more than sixty years it had been the highway to the West—long before canals and steam railroads were thought of. The big canvas-topped wagons still hauled freight over it, and there were farms and settlements scattered along its dusty length.

The woods along the canal had been cut off years ago, and now bushes and half-grown saplings stood among the stumps. What lay beyond, Jonathan did not know. But the sooner he made a start, the sooner he would get to some kind of civilization. He got to his feet, took a rough bearing by the stars and set off through the brush on a course that bore straight away from the tow-path.

It was rough going, up hill and down. He fell over stumps and bruised his shins on rocks. Once, when he had been going a long time and was almost at the limit of his strength, he fell headfirst into a swamp-hole. The black, evil-smelling water and the yielding mud that sucked at his arms and legs threw him into a panic of fear. Gasping, he fought his way to a clump of birch saplings and dragged himself free.

There was higher ground ahead. After a moment's rest, he staggered around the edge of the little swamp and began climbing. Near the top of the ridge he came to a clump of bushy young pine trees and felt a soft, deep carpet of pine needles under his feet. He was very, very tired. He dropped to his knees and lay down with a sigh. In the next breath he was asleep, dreaming of his own clean, comfortable bed back in the Pine Tree State.

# EIGHT

THE SUN WAS NEARLY AN HOUR HIGH WHEN THE BOY OPENED his eyes. Trying to move, he felt a painful stiffness in his legs and a hollow ache at the pit of his stomach. He hauled himself erect and looked down ruefully at his scarecrow costume. His clothes had dried on him. They were wrinkled and plastered with mud and pine needles, and his boots looked like lumps of dry clay. His cap had been left behind on the Pioneer packet, and when he passed a hand over his matted hair, a showcr of sticks and leaves fell from his head.

He was trying to comb out his locks with his fingers when

a faint fragrance came over the ridge on the morning breeze. Jonathan stiffened like a pointer dog, for the scent was unmistakable—the mouth-watering smell of frying bacon!

He hurried over the crest of the hill and down through the woods on the other side. In a moment he saw a wisp of smoke rising from a campfire. Among the trees stood a queer-looking covered wagon with a square black top. And bending over the fire, frying-pan in hand, was a little, roly-poly man in a rusty black tail-coat.

The man was bareheaded and his long white hair hung like a mane almost to his shoulders. He turned his face toward Jonathan as the boy approached. There was something friendly and childlike about his smile, even though his eyes were hidden by green spectacles.

"Good morning!" he called in a gentle, musical voice. "Join me in some bacon and eggs?"

"G-gosh, mister," Jonathan choked. "I'd sure be grateful. Sorry I'm so messy-looking, but I—I lost my way in the night and fell in a mudhole."

The man nodded gravely. "Your appearance can't possibly offend me," he replied. "That's one of the special advantages of having no eyes. You see," he added simply, "I'm blind."

"Oh," breathed Jonathan, "I—I didn't know—"

"There's a stream down yonder, if you'd like to clean up a bit," the little man suggested. "Meanwhile I'll put some more of these homely viands in the skillet."

Jonathan washed at the brook. On the way back he stopped a moment, staring at the covered wagon. On its black canvas side were neatly painted words:

THE TRAVELING ATHENAEUM

*Books Bought & Sold*
*Letters Written*

NATHANIEL GREENFIELD

Curious, the boy walked past the rear end of the vehicle and peered in under the curtain. Both sides were lined with shelves on which stood hundreds of books—more books than Jonathan had ever seen gathered in one place before. The space between was filled by a neatly made-up bed, laid on the floor boards.

The wagon's shafts stood empty and there was no sign of a horse anywhere about.

The aroma of the bacon was too tempting to let the boy loiter any longer. He hurried back to the fire.

"Our repast is about ready," announced the blind man. "You'll find another plate and a fork in the box under the wagon seat."

Jonathan was so busy devouring his breakfast that he had no leisure to talk in the next few minutes. And his host tactfully refrained from asking questions. The boy noticed that he ate slowly but with the greatest neatness. When he transferred food from the skillet to the plate his fork made little exploratory movements, locating the rashers of bacon that remained, counting them by touch, then lifting one with a delicate skill that was beautiful to watch.

"I think," said the little man, at length, "that you must have been pretty hungry."

"Yes," Jonathan told him. "The last meal I had was day before yesterday—at noon."

Concern showed on the other's round, pink face, and he pursed his lips in a silent whistle. "That's bad," he said. "Very bad. I doubt if I could stand it. As you can see from my figure I get great comfort out of eating."

"I looked at the sign on your wagon," said Jonathan. "Are you Mr. Greenfield, the bookseller?"

"Quite correct," the little man beamed. "I took up the occupation some ten years ago, after losing my sight. Books had always been my hobby as well as my livelihood, for at one time I was a publisher in a small way. The 'Traveling Athenaeum' was an idea that appealed to me, and it's provided me a very fair living. Also, I feel that the dissemination of reading matter among the poor country folk, far from centers of culture, is a worthy career, however humble it may seem."

Jonathan listened to the big words open-mouthed. He knew what most of them meant, but it was the pride and sincerity behind them that really impressed him. There was something appealing about the gentle-voiced little man.

"I have no wish to pry into your affairs," Mr. Greenfield continued, "but I take it you must be in some difficulty. I would be truly glad if there were any way in which I might assist you."

Jonathan told his story as briefly as he could. "All I could think of," he said, "after I got out of the canal, was to head for the Conestoga Road. I suppose it isn't too far from here."

"Roughly a quarter of a mile," Mr. Greenfield smiled. "I asked Enoch to turn off and find a camping spot and he drove in here."

"Enoch?" asked the boy.

"He's the country lad who has been doing my driving for me. I'd had him two weeks. But I paid him after supper last night and perhaps that was a mistake. The next time I called to him he didn't answer. I fear," he sighed, "the boy had been a trifle homesick."

"He didn't take your horse with him, did he?" asked Jonathan.

"My horse? Old Dolly? Gracious me, I hope not!" cried the bookseller, startled. He rose and put two fingers to his lips, giving forth a piercing whistle.

They listened and in a moment there was a thud of hoofs beyond the brook. A fat old gray mare came across the clearing at a lumbering trot.

"Here, Dolly—good Dolly—that's my girl!" cooed the little man in obvious relief.

Jonathan watched his sensitive fingers caress the mare's velvety nose.

"Mr. Greenfield," he said hesitantly, "do you—could you, maybe, use a new driver? That is, if you're headed the same way I am?"

"Exactly what I was about to propose," the man replied eagerly. "It happens that I am headed westward—to Pittsburgh, in fact, and possibly out through Ohio. We may not travel as fast as the express boats on the canal, but we get there—don't we, eh, Dolly? Besides, anyone who drives for me is apt to eat three meals a day. That may be something to consider."

"Yes," Jonathan grinned. "Guess I was thinking of that, too. I wouldn't want any wages, just so I could earn my board along the road."

"Two dollars a week and found," the bookseller answered with firmness. "That's what I paid Enoch and others before him. You'll earn it, my boy. By the way, do you read aloud?"

"Well, fair, I reckon. Nothing extra, but I've been through the Sixth Reader in school back home."

Greenfield nodded. "I confess Enoch was a bit of a disappointment," said he. "I enjoy having somebody read to me, and Enoch's efforts were not of the best. If it's agreed that you're now in my employ, what say we make a start?"

"Fine!" said the boy. "I'll hustle these dishes down to the brook an' be back in a jiffy."

He scrubbed the skillet bottom with fine sand and washed the plates and forks. In the wagon-box he found a clean flour sack which he used to dry them. And when they had been stowed away he put the harness on the gray mare and hitched her up.

Mr. Greenfield climbed up to the seat and Jonathan took his place beside him, reins in hand. He was looking around for the track by which the wagon must have entered the clearing.

"Right over that way," said the blind man, pointing to the left.

"You mean you can—you *know* the way?" asked the boy, astonished.

"I have a pretty good sense of direction," Greenfield chuckled. "If you hadn't appeared so opportunely, I suppose I'd have driven out of here myself, with some help from Dolly."

In a few minutes they were on the turnpike and headed toward the distant blue ridges of the Alleghenies. The old mare struck a plodding gait somewhere between a walk and a trot and held it steadily, mile after mile. There was little for Jonathan to do but hold the reins and listen to the plump bookseller's rambling conversation.

"You may well wonder," Mr. Greenfield said, "how an itinerant peddler of books keeps body and soul together in these wilderness districts. Truth is, there's hardly a farmhouse or trapper's cabin betwixt Philadelphia and the Wabash that hasn't a book in it bought from my stock. Surprisingly enough, it's not just the Bible and the 'Farmer's Almanac' they buy, either. Many a copy of the 'Decline and Fall' I've sold, and 'Plutarch's Lives,' and even texts in Greek and Latin. Cooper's novels are favorites, of course, and Scott's, and some of Parson Weems' writings. The good parson, by the way, sold books from a wagon, much as I do. His 'Life of Washington' is still one of my better-selling volumes."

Jonathan's head whirled with all these authors' names and book titles. One or two of Cooper's romances he had read, but beyond that he was lost.

"How much do books bring when you sell 'em?" he ventured.

"Depends on the book," the little man explained. "Some, like the 'Almanac' or the 'Brief Compendium of Veterinary Medicine,' I sell for ten cents or a quarter. The 'Complete Shakespeare' is worth four dollars. I don't always get paid in cash, of course. Eggs and bacon and potatoes and an occasional chicken are welcome in trade. And sometimes I take in a prime beaver-skin."

An alert look came over the little man's face and he held

up a finger, as if listening. "Didn't I hear a dog bark?" he asked. "There should be a settlement near if I remember right, and a dog usually means people. Do you see anything?"

Jonathan, too, caught the faint yapping of a dog. But it was not until they topped the next hill that he reported a little group of houses clustered by the road ahead.

"Ah," said the bookseller. "Must be Burksville. Fine—I sold a Milton's 'Paradise Lost' to the tavern-keeper here last year."

He clambered back into the cavern of the wagon body and reappeared with a battered silk hat on his long white locks.

Jonathan drove up in front of the only two-story building in the hamlet and stopped the mare. Two or three loafers came out on the puncheon stoop to stare at the new arrivals.

"Wal," called one of the men, "durned if it ain't the Perfessor! Hey, Mike, come out here. Ye said ye was itchin' to buy a book! Now's yer chance."

The "Perfessor" smiled and bowed and climbed down over the wheel. A burly man in a white apron came out of the tavern, wiping his hands.

"Begorra," he roared, " 'tis glad I am to see yez, or me name ain't Mike Burk! Still peddlin' the books?"

"Indeed I am, sir," laughed the little man. "And I hope

you've enjoyed the one you bought last summer?"

Burk flushed and hung his head. "To be honest wid yez," he stammered, "the wurrds in it was too much fer me. I been usin' it fer a door weight. A foine big book it is, but have ye got somethin' a bit more in me own line?"

The bookseller took off his hat and scratched his head. "Let me see, let me see," he murmured. "Ah, yes! The very thing!"

He scampered to the back of the wagon, pulled down the folding step and climbed into the dark interior. Looking back from the driver's seat, Jonathan could see his sensitive fingers feeling along the rows of books. In a moment he pulled out a small, cloth-bound volume.

"Here you are, friend Burk!" he cried jubilantly, as he descended to the road again. "This book is called 'The Complete Tavern-Keeper.' It has chapters on the making of punches of all kinds, recipes for venison pasties, instructions for broiling steaks and polishing brass, and excellent advice on the mending of bed sheets. Only one dollar, sir, and the book is yours!"

Burk took the volume from his hand and fumbled over the pages. "Faith," he said, "if all them things is in it, the book's a fair bargain. Will ye have it in cash or in meals fer yerself an' the lad?"

"Meaning no offense to your fine table," replied the little man, "I think I would prefer coin of the realm."

The innkeeper chuckled good-naturedly and pulled a greenback out of his pocket. "I'll not be wantin' me money back fer the 'Paradise' book," he said. "Wid the heft of it, 'tis better than a brick fer holdin' doors. An' it gives a bit of a high-toned air to the place!"

Mr. Greenfield made several more sales in the little settlement before they drove on. Two housewives bought cookbooks, and a tall, bearded Scotch-Irish farmer from the back clearings stopped the van to purchase a copy of "Rob Roy."

With two dollars in cash, and their larder increased by four dozen eggs and a big loaf of home-made bread, the bookseller and his new driver moved on some ten miles farther before nightfall.

"You'll have to tell me, Jonathan, when it begins to grow dark," Mr. Greenfield reminded the boy. "I can sometimes tell by the feel of the wind, or the sound of the birds, but my idea of time isn't perfect by any means."

"Well," said Jonathan, "I should judge it's 'round six o'clock now. Sky's clouding up a mite, so it'll be dark early. I reckon old Dolly's getting tired, too. Want me to start watching for a place to spend the night?"

"By all means," replied the little man. "A farmhouse might be best if we are likely to have rain."

The road at that point was a rutted track leading upward along a wooded hillside. Jonathan had seen no farms in the last mile or more, but there was a drift of smoke above the trees ahead, and he urged the mare to quicken her plodding pace.

The smoke came from the chimney of a weather-beaten log house that sat forlornly in the middle of a clearing. A big black hound dog got up from the doorsill and bayed as the wagon turned in.

"Hello, the house!" Jonathan shouted. "Anybody home?"

At that, the puncheon door opened and a short, bowed figure was silhouetted against the firelight within. It was a very old man with a flowing white beard.

"Who be ye?" came his quavering voice. "Who be ye, an' what d' ye want?"

"It's Mr. Greenfield, the bookseller," Jonathan answered. "I'm his driver. Could you put us up tonight?"

The old man peered at the wagon and its occupants as they drew nearer. "Reckon so," he said at last. "I'll put a couple more 'taters on the coals. Ye kin tie yer hoss up in the shed, out back."

# NINE

IT WAS BEGINNING TO SPRINKLE AS THE BOY UNHITCHED DOLLY and led her into an empty pole lean-to behind the cabin. He found some old straw, to make her a bed, and brought a measure of grain from the wagon. His employer meanwhile was fastening the canvas cover tight against the weather.

At Mr. Greenfield's suggestion, Jonathan carried a dozen eggs when they returned to the front of the house.

Their host watched Jonathan guide the little bookseller over the threshold and his bushy eyebrows went up.

"What ails the feller?" he asked. "Can't he see good?"

"That's right, friend," Mr. Greenfield told him with a smile. "I'm blind. It's most kind of you to give us shelter from the elements. Jonathan—present our small offering."

"Eggs, eh?" piped the ancient man. "Good 'nuff. Ain't et a egg all winter. Bobcats got my banty hen. Set ye down whiles I git the vittles ready."

They sat on a half-log bench and Jonathan looked about him. The cabin was crudely furnished but neat as a pin. The hearth was well brushed, the ax-hewn floor clean, and such utensils as there were had been hung in orderly array. An ancient, long-barreled Pennsylvania rifle rested on buckhorns above the big fireplace.

The old backwoodsman was bustling about like a squirrel. With his wrinkled face and vast, snowy beard, his bent back and gnarled, veined hands, he looked at least eighty. Yet his motions were as spry as those of a much younger man.

He turned once and caught the boy's curious eyes on him.

"Mebbe," he said, "ye don't know who I am—bein' strangers to these parts. Folks 'round here calls me Uncle Billy. Right name's William Flood. Been here durn nigh sence the flood, too! Heh-heh!"

His gleeful cackle filled the little house and brought the hound to the door, whining and scratching to be admitted.

There was a proud gleam in the old man's eye as he hobbled over to let the dog in.

"Yessir," he announced, "I teamed 'long this road fer forty year. Druv 'stogie wagons back in the days when that was th' onliest way to git stuff over the mountings."

He came back to the fire, filled three pewter plates with side meat and dandelion greens and fished three baked potatoes out of the ashes.

The old fellow mumbled his food between toothless gums but he seemed to be enjoying every mouthful.

"You must have been around here back in Indian days, Mr. Flood," Jonathan ventured.

"Injun days? Heck, sonny, 'fore I was yore age I'd done sculped half a dozen o' the varmints. My paw an' maw was massacreed up in the Wyomin' Valley in 'seventy-eight. I was jest a sprout of a boy but I done got me a rifle an' a hatchet an' took out arter 'em with the scouts. We trailed the devils halfway to Canady, pickin' 'em off one by one."

The mild little bookseller was flushed with excitement. "What a life you must have led!" he exclaimed. "Like Cooper's Natty Bumppo. No doubt you've read the 'Leatherstocking' tales?"

"Readin' an' writin' ain't in my line," said Flood scornfully. "All I want to read is sign—deer an' b'ar an' Injun sign. Books is a plumb waste of eyesight."

Mr. Greenfield's apple face puckered in distress. "I must disagree with you there, my friend," he replied. "Reading, I sincerely believe, is one of the noblest gifts the good Lord has given us. Only a man who has lost the power to read can fully appreciate it."

"Wal," said the old woodsman uncomfortably, "mebbe so—mebbe so. I've got on tol'able well without it fer more'n eighty year, though."

Looking about for a topic of conversation that would be more agreeable, Jonathan complimented the ex-Indian-fighter on the neatness of his abode. "Looks as spick-and-span as if you had a woman keeping house for you," he remarked.

"Woman?" snorted Flood. "Bah! Wouldn't hev no woman messin' round no cabin o' mine. I set out to git married oncet, when I was young an' foolish, but I was lucky. Gal run off with a pack-peddler."

The rain beat on the roof and hissed in the chimney-throat. There was no more talk for a while. Uncle Billy Flood sat on a hickory stool by the hearth and fondled the black hound's ears.

"Nope," he said at length, "don't need no woman to take keer of us. Ol' Big Mouth here an' me, we git along. He keeps the varmints down an' I manage to keep us in meat, what with a hog or two an' deer an' wild turkey. Ain't much else we need."

He paused to throw another log on the fire, then went on. "Hed some money oncet. Kep' me 'wake nights worryin' over it. Figger I'm better off like I am."

"What happened to it—the money, I mean?" asked Jonathan.

"Eh? Oh, the money. That was a couple o' year back. I'd saved up 'most eight hunderd dollars—been savin' it ever since my teamin' days. Feller on hoss-back come through here, one night, an' I let him sleep in the cabin. Durn if he didn't rob me!"

The old man sounded so disgusted that Jonathan was afraid he wouldn't finish the story. "What sort of man was he?" he prompted.

"Red-headed feller in town clothes," growled Flood, spitting into the ashes. "I hed the money in a sack under a loose brick yonder." He indicated one of the hearth bricks with his moccasined toe.

"Took special pains to stomp on it an' kick ashes in the crack so's he wouldn't notice it was loose. He et supper with me nice as pie an' I give him a buff'ler robe to sleep on. Both'n us went to sleep—leastways he was snorin'—but arter a spell I woke up. Heered the door hinge creak. I jumped fer my rifle but the feller was too quick. Time I got out in the clearin' he was gallopin' off, an' my shot didn't drap him like it orter. Must ha' been almighty close, though. 'Pears like he'd lifted the brick an' took the money."

"Did you ever find out who he was?" asked Jonathan. As the tale unfolded he had begun to have a prickly feeling at the back of his neck. "You said the man was red-headed and wore town clothes. Any special kind of clothes?"

"Hm," said the old teamster. "If I ain't mistook he had on a big black hat an' a green sort o' coat. Folks in Burksville claimed he was a reg'lar highwayman—wanted fer robbin' a stage, somewheres over on the Monongahela. Name o' McKee."

The boy drew a deep breath and leaned back, thoughtful.

Mr. Greenfield cleared his throat. "After entertaining such a scoundrel," he said, "I should think you would hesitate before taking in strangers."

"Nope," the old man replied grimly. "Ain't got nothin' to steal. More'n that—you see that rifle? She's loaded an' primed. An' I've trained ol' Big Mouth here to make a fuss if there's any queer goin's-on. Nope, I ain't feared o' nobody."

A few minutes later he climbed a ladder to the loft and threw down a couple of mangy-looking buffalo hides.

"Thar's yer beds," he told his guests. "Sleep comf'table."

Jonathan led Mr. Greenfield over to his hairy couch and went to his own, while the old woodsman crawled into the single bunk against the wall.

The fire died down to dull red embers and the hound dog twitched and snored on the hearth. Jonathan lay there thinking for a long time before he got to sleep.

. . .

The rain had stopped before daylight. When the boy stretched and sat up he saw an early sunbeam coming through the cabin's one window. The old woodsman was crouching over a fresh-built fire, stirring porridge in an iron pot.

Jonathan's "good morning" was answered by a non-committal grunt. He woke his employer and took him outside to wash by the well. When he had watered and fed the mare, their frugal breakfast was ready—porridge with black-strap molasses and tea.

Mr. Greenfield offered to pay for the night's lodging but the old man refused. "Don't want no money layin' around," he said. "Nothin' but trouble comes of it. When folks look honest an' the weather's bad outside I'm glad to hev 'em in. But I don't run no ho-tel."

They thanked him and drove off, moving slowly through the ruts, now deep with mud.

"Quite a character," chuckled the bookseller. "I'd have slept far more comfortably in my own bed in the wagon but I didn't want to hurt Mr. Flood's feelings. Also we'll stop after a bit and eat a real breakfast. Tell me, my boy—

was I wrong in thinking you had a special interest in our friend's account of the robbery?"

"Why—no, sir," said Jonathan. "Remember I told you somebody stole my money in New York? Well, it was the same man. It was McKee. He had a scar at the side of his mouth. Mr. Flood didn't mention seeing it, but maybe he shot straighter than he thought, that night."

"Well, well!" the little man exclaimed. "It's all quite disturbing, isn't it? When I think of the years I've traveled these roads, I wonder why I've never encountered any really wicked people. Not that I'd be worth robbing for my money, but there are the books! Perhaps men of McKee's stripe never realize what riches there are between the covers of books. Or perhaps a special Providence takes care of helpless people."

They covered only about ten miles by noon because of the mud, but after a picnic lunch by the roadside they found firmer going. A few books were sold at isolated farmhouses, but they came to no towns. Toward evening Jonathan told the blind man that he could see a high mountain ridge not far ahead. It loomed up before them suddenly as they came over a hilltop.

"Yes," said Mr. Greenfield with a sigh. "It's time we were getting to the mountains. I always dread the hard pulling, and so does poor Dolly, no doubt. Still, that's what life is—ups and downs. Once we're over we'll have it downhill for quite a while."

They camped in a little valley close to the mountain's foot. After supper Jonathan washed some of his clothes in a creek that ran past under the bridge and hung them on a bush to dry. Rolled up in a blanket on a bed of ferns he could watch the stars wheel by overhead. It was, he decided, a considerable improvement over the sleeping arrangements of the night before.

The morning dawned clear, and they were on their way by seven o'clock. As they neared the foot of the mountain, Jonathan saw a white church steeple and a cluster of houses.

He asked his companion what town it was, and Mr. Greenfield rubbed his chin thoughtfully.

"I believe it's Hollidaysburg," he said. "Do you see something like a railroad going up the side of the mountain?"

Jonathan shaded his eyes and studied the wooded slope. "Yes," he replied. "It looks like a double line of tracks. And there's something going up now! My gosh! It's a pair of railroad carriages!"

As he watched, the two coaches, coupled together, and looking no bigger than beetles at that distance, crawled slowly higher. And from the crest of the ridge a similar pair of cars came creeping down the other track to meet and pass them.

"It must be an interesting sight," said the little bookseller with a sigh. "I'm told it's done by cables and steam-engines, with one train acting as a counterweight to the other—just like two buckets in a well."

These, thought Jonathan, must be the "planes" he had heard about—where the canal-boat passengers were carried in coaches straight up a thousand-foot mountainside. He watched, fascinated, until roadside trees cut off his view.

Hollidaysburg proved to be a pleasant, bustling little town with a prosperous air. Well-built houses and attractive yards lined its principal street. Mr. Greenfield donned his top hat and prepared for business.

That was a profitable morning. The Presbyterian minister not only bought half a dozen volumes himself, but suggested the names of several other townspeople who made purchases. The bookseller was in high spirits and his pockets jingled with silver when they started up the mountain after an early midday meal.

The road climbed and zigzagged for miles, never going straight up the slope but twisting back and forth like a snake track. Old Dolly labored up the grades, willing enough, but blowing and sweating. Jonathan walked beside her. Every little while he chocked the wagon wheel with a rock and gave the mare a chance to rest. Mr. Greenfield also got down from the seat and panted up the hill on foot, encouraging Dolly with such loving words as he had breath for.

They had been climbing for nearly three hours when they reached a rocky ledge well up toward the summit. There was a fairly level spot where the road made one of its sudden switchbacks, and Jonathan led his employer over to a rock where he could sit down. Below them lay mile on mile of rugged country, stretching away to the eastern horizon. The boy was admiring all this wild grandeur when a horse whinnied close by. Dolly lifted her head and wheezed an answer.

It took Jonathan a moment or two to locate the other animal. It was not on the road but tied to a tree on the slope above them—a big, rangy roan wearing a silver-mounted saddle.

"Hello, down there!" came a hail from still farther up the mountainside, and a tall young man came sliding down through the brush.

"Nat Greenfield!" he whooped. "You old bookworm, how in the world did you get up here?"

The little man scrambled to his feet, his face glowing. "Tom—Tom Cole—is that you?" he asked. "Come here, where I can get my hands on you!"

There was genuine affection in their greeting. Jonathan watched it, shy and a little envious. He liked the young man's looks. He had the air of a gentleman, yet he was dressed in rough hunting clothes, briar-torn and faded. His face was bronzed by the sun, and when he smiled there were crinkles of merriment at the corners of his brown eyes.

The two men were talking and laughing, asking questions, interrupting each other. Jonathan had turned away and was pitching pebbles down the hill when the bookseller called his name.

"Come and shake hands with my friend Thomas Cole," he said. "One of America's great painters-to-be. Tom, this lad came to me like manna from heaven when my last driver took French leave. He's my eyes and my right arm."

Cole looked Jonathan up and down appraisingly. He seemed satisfied, for his face broke into an engaging grin.

"It's a pleasure to meet you, sir," he said, and the boy returned the compliment.

"My easel's up there on the ledge," the painter told them. "I'm trying to catch the sweep of this view, and the cloud shadows moving over the forest. I'd like to finish my sketch while the light's good. Where do you plan to camp?"

"We'll push on over the mountain," the blind man replied. "If I'm not mistaken, there's a spring a mile or two beyond the crest, and we'll try to reach it before dark."

"Fine!" nodded Cole. "I'll overtake you there." And he bounded away up the hillside.

# TEN

THERE WAS A MOUNTAIN CHILL IN THE AIR AFTER SUNSET, AND Jonathan fed the fire with dry wood till the little glade was cheerful with light and warmth. The last pull over the top of the gap had been hard on the fat old mare. The boy rubbed her down and put a blanket on her before supper.

Since they were expecting company, the little bookseller made extra preparations for the meal. Chuckling with pleasure, he cut up a plump hen to stew in the pot, his sensitive fingers moving quickly and surely. Jonathan always marveled when he watched the blind man about his housekeeping tasks. He kept the wagon as neat as a New England parlor, and he was a far better cook than the boy ever hoped to be.

It was almost dark, and the hoot owls were calling in the woods, when Tom Cole rode up to the fireside on his tall roan.

He swung down with a hearty hail and stood warming his hands by the fire.

"How did your painting go?" Mr. Greenfield asked.

"Only fair, I'd say," replied the big young man. "The colors are there and I can see 'em, but they're never as lovely on canvas—at least when I'm holding the brush."

He frowned a little. "It's discouraging when I see how far short of nature I am. Some of the fellows in the Hudson Valley are coming closer though. If I keep on another ten years I hope I can do something really worth while."

"Could I see it—the painting, I mean?" asked Jonathan shyly.

"Why, of course," the artist agreed. "It won't look like much by firelight, but I'm glad to show it to you." He unbuckled a tarpaulin-covered wooden frame that was strapped to two rings in the cantle of the handsome saddle.

It was an ingenious contrivance, holding a light, folding easel, a palette, brushes and a box of paint tubes, and half a dozen small canvases on stretchers. One at a time he held the color sketches so that the flickering light from the fire fell on them.

"I know that place!" cried Jonathan. "That's the Susquehanna below the long bridge at Harrisburg. And this one—isn't it the canal?"

"Right," said Cole. "And here's the one I was working on this afternoon. Careful—it isn't dry yet."

"Gee," the boy breathed, "it's beautiful! It looks as if you could see a hundred miles. And that wagon on the road below—why, that's our wagon—and old Dolly!"

"Think of that!" exclaimed the bookseller happily. "How I wish I could see it! We'll be famous yet, Jonathan."

That was the merriest meal the Maine boy had enjoyed since he left his friends on the *Phoebe Foster*. Tom Cole was a well-read young man and it was a pleasure to hear him discuss books with his old friend. Mr. Greenfield asked his opinion on many of the newer literary works and filed the comments away in his amazing memory.

"All the old books I've read for myself," he laughed ruefully. "But anything that's been published since I lost my eyes is *terra incognita*. If you've never studied Latin, my boy," he explained to Jonathan, "that means 'unknown country.' "

"I expect you'll sell a lot of books by this chap Dickens—or 'Boz,' as they call him," said Cole. "He was being quoted by everybody when I left New York. 'Pickwick Papers' is one of the funniest things I ever read. They say his account of his visit to America is making a lot of folks hopping mad, though. Takes a fall out of our tobacco-spitting congressmen in Washington. For my part I don't blame him. Always thought it was a filthy habit. But the place where he really touches us on the raw is the slavery question. Some of these hot-headed Southerners plan to boycott him from now on!"

"There are sad, troubled times ahead, I fear," the little bookseller sighed. "I used to love the South and had many friends there—Richmond—Charleston—Savannah. I suppose I'll never visit them again."

"Pshaw!" said Cole, patting his friend's shoulder. "It isn't that bad. Too many sensible people, North and South, to let things get out of hand. If this fuss about the Mexican border grows much worse, we'll all forget the slavery problem and go marching off to a war together."

"Dear me, I hope not!" cried the older man in dismay. "All that suffering and dying, just for a river in the middle of a cactus desert! I knew a man who'd been in Texas. Said it was a forsaken kind of country and he couldn't imagine why Houston and Crockett and the rest wanted it in the first place.

"Besides," he went on, "wars upset everything. I remember the last one—the war with the British that ended in 'fifteen. After it was over the roads were full of vagabonds and bandits. Some claimed they'd fought under General Jackson and hadn't been paid. Others were just restless rogues looking for easy pickings. Times are always bad after a war."

Tom Cole laughed. "I wouldn't call times like these too settled," he said. "The law keeps things in hand in the cities, and the farm districts are peaceful enough. But here in the mountains and in the western frontier settlements there are plenty of rough characters. Why, I—well, never mind."

"What were you going to say, Tom?" the bookseller asked quietly.

"Nothing much. I didn't want to start you worrying. I was just going to say I wouldn't like to travel this road with very much money in my purse. When I left Harrisburg last week the news was that some fellow in a mask had held up a mail coach—the one that runs from York to Lancaster. Got away with more than a thousand dollars.

"Of course," he added, "nobody's going to rob a poor painter. And I doubt if they'd bother you, either. Still, it might be a good idea if Jonathan had a gun or a pistol. Can you shoot, son?"

"Yes," said Jonathan. "Never tried with a pistol, but I—"

"Now, now," Mr. Greenfield interrupted, "I'm not in the least alarmed, Tom. Look at the years I've traveled around these parts, and never any trouble. I don't care for the idea of firearms in the Traveling Athenaeum, either. No telling when I might step on a gun and set it off!"

Jonathan, who had been picturing himself in the role of armed protector, felt a little disappointed. Tom Cole, on the other hand, seemed satisfied to let the matter drop. They chatted for another hour, and it was not until the tall young painter was rolled up in his blanket next to Jonathan's that he mentioned the subject again.

"I wasn't talking nonsense—about the gun," he whispered cautiously. "Nat's such a good, trusting soul he wouldn't believe anybody'd ever think of robbing him. But you'll be going through some rough country. I wish I could travel along and keep you company, but I can't. So take this and keep it in your pocket. It's up to you to take care of him."

He handed the boy a small pistol and a leather sack of powder and ball.

"I'll do my best," Jonathan whispered back.

After that there was no sound in the mountain night but the crackle of the dying embers and the faint, far-off yowl of a bobcat. It took the boy a long time to get to sleep.

. . .

They started again in the misty dawn, and Cole rode beside the wagon as far as the first settlement—a log tavern and half a dozen houses in a steep-sided little valley a few miles beyond the gap. There he left them. He had heard of a picturesque spot in the mountains to the southward that might be worth painting, and he rode off on his big roan horse, waving them a cheery farewell.

"Look me up if you ever get to New York, Jonathan," he called. "They'll know where I am at the Knickerbocker Club."

Jonathan shouted back that he would, but he had his own doubts. Since he was on his way to live in the distant prairies of Illinois it seemed highly improbable that he would ever see the young artist again.

They found little demand for books in the settlement. Only one or two of the inhabitants knew how to read, and a single copy of the "Brief Compendium of Veterinary Medicine," sold to the local blacksmith, was the total of their business for the day.

There were several more mountain ranges to cross, but the slopes were more gradual now, and the road ran fairly straight through the forest.

"I always have a feeling of relief at this point of the journey," the little bookseller remarked. "The worst is behind us, and the best ahead. What say we improve our minds a bit? Dolly can't miss her way here, and there are books I should know better. You'll find a copy of 'Pickwick Papers' back there on the right—third shelf, I believe.

Let's find out how well you read."

Jonathan found the volume and returned with it to the driver's seat.

" 'Chapter One. The Pickwickians,' " he began. " 'The first ray of light which illumines the gloom, and converts into dazzling brilliancy that obscurity in which the earlier history of the public career of the immortal Pickwick would appear to be involved, is derived from the perusal of the following entry in the Transactions of the Pickwick Club.' "

He knew he was making heavy weather of some of the big words, but Mr. Greenfield nodded encouragingly.

"Keep on," smiled the little man. "I'll give you assistance if you find one you can't pronounce, but you're much better at it than Enoch was."

So Jonathan labored on. He didn't get much sense out of the first few pages, but when he came to the battle with the cab-driver, the rescue by Mr. Jingle and the adventures which followed, he began to be really interested. Several times, before the afternoon was over, he sat back and laughed as heartily as his employer.

In the next two days they came to think of the genial Mr. Pickwick, Sam Weller and the Fat Boy as old friends. Before they came in sight of the Monongahela and the western settlements, Jonathan had read himself hoarse several times over, and had finished not only "Pickwick" but

"Sketches by Boz" and "Oliver Twist."

It was fine June weather when the wagon rolled down out of the foothills. For the first time since they crossed the mountains, they were in thickly populated country. Villages and towns crowded each other along the banks of the rivers. Sawmills, boat yards and whisky distilleries were bustling with activity.

These were still the foremost industries of the region, though at night the sky was beginning to glow with the ruddy light from scattered iron furnaces and forges.

"Folks around here seem mighty busy," Jonathan remarked, as they drove along the river bank. "I don't think much o' the flatboats they build—they're tubby enough compared to our Kennebec ships—but they hammer together a lot of 'em. There were fifteen hulls in that yard we just passed."

"Yes," said the bookseller. "The movers still use flatboats to take their goods down the Ohio. But it's not like the old days. More folks travel by steamboat now, and others go on by wagon, since the roads are better. You're right, though, about its being a busy place. Everybody's making money."

"Then I guess we can sell a lot of books," the boy suggested.

"Well," Mr. Greenfield answered, "I'm afraid we can't count on it. You see, when people spend all their days making money, they don't have time for reading. In another generation, no doubt, the towns hereabouts will have a leisure class and understand cultural pursuits. Today their tastes run more to horse races, rough-and-tumble fighting and Monongahela red-eye."

Actually, business turned out a little better than they had expected. When they camped for the night a few miles above Pittsburgh, a caravan of wagons pulled into the grove near them and a tall, gray, scholarly-looking man came over to their fire. In his black clothes he looked like a parson.

"Your pardon, gentlemen," he said in a fine resonant voice. "The inscription on your vehicle attracted me. I had hardly expected to encounter a fount of learning in this distressing wilderness. In some unaccountable fashion I have mislaid my volume of Sophocles. Is it possible that you might have a copy of the Greek text in your Athenaeum?"

The little bookseller had risen from his frying-pan and bowed in the direction of the stranger. "Quite possible," he beamed. "I am Nathaniel Greenfield, at your service, sir."

"I should have introduced myself," said the tall man. "Eliphalet Carter, late of Amherst College, now on my way with a group of other teachers and their families to Bloomington, Indiana, site of the new state university."

He followed Mr. Greenfield to the van and soon completed the purchase of his Sophocles. Before the evening ended, several of his learned companions came over to browse among the wagon's shelves. The "Athenaeum" took in six or seven dollars that night.

Visiting the neighboring group of wagons after supper, Jonathan made the acquaintance of the younger members of the party. Some of the professors had big families, ranging from his own age and older down to tots hardly able to walk. It was good to hear real New England accents again.

Noah Carter, sixteen-year-old son of the dignified Eliphalet, turned out to be a lively, freckle-faced youngster with no trace of his father's stiffness. He was keenly interested in Jonathan's adventures.

"I guess we'd have been robbed a dozen times over on this trip," he said, "if we had anything worth taking. Most of the cargo in our wagons is dusty old books and a little furniture. There isn't a gun in the whole crowd, nor a man that would know how to shoot one. How are you going to travel from Pittsburgh on?"

"I'll stay with Mr. Greenfield, I reckon," Jonathan told him. "Old Dolly isn't fast but she gets there. And I'd feel sort of mean if I left 'em now."

The other boy nodded. "We're taking the steamboat down as far as New Albany," he said. "I thought maybe you'd like to go along."

"That would be mighty nice if I could afford it," Jonathan replied. "Somebody's got to look after the old gentleman though, and as long as he's heading my way I'll keep my job."

"Well," Noah Carter grinned, "see you out West. Maybe we can go buffalo hunting together—or fighting Indians. Indiana and Illinois are next-door neighbors, according to the map."

They said good-night and Jonathan went back to the wagon and his blanket. He wondered if he had decided right. Traveling by the river might shorten his trip by a week or two. But he remembered his promise to Tom Cole that he would take care of the blind bookseller, and went to sleep with a clear conscience.

# ELEVEN

THEY ENTERED PITTSBURGH AN HOUR AFTER BREAKFAST THE next morning. It was a big town, sprawled along the lower ground that formed a triangular point between the rivers. Back of it were high, wooded bluffs. Its rutted streets were filled with movers' wagons, and its waterfront lined with steamboats, barges and flatboats. Trade in the stores and taverns was brisk, for Pittsburgh was still the main gateway to the Ohio Valley towns and the new frontiers beyond. Migrating families by the thousands passed through it every year.

"We'll try the ministers first," said Mr. Greenfield briskly. "They haven't much money, but they're readers. Head for the first church steeple you see."

By noon they had visited the pastors of four different churches, ranging from a long-faced Scottish dominie who wanted nothing but theological works to a plump and genial Episcopalian rector with a lively taste in romantic novels. This gentleman not only invited them to luncheon but suggested the names of a dozen parishioners who had literary leanings.

That evening they put up at a modest boarding-house where Mr. Greenfield had stayed before. It was part way up the bluff and its wide wooden porch gave Jonathan a fine view of the city and the rivers. They sat there in the sunset and discussed the day's work.

The bookseller passed his worn leather purse over to Jonathan. "I wish you'd count it for me," he said. "Paper money is hard on a man with no eyes. I can make change and count coins as fast as anyone, but the notes all feel alike. As nearly as I can figure we ought to have about a hundred and ninety dollars."

"A hundred an' ninety-two an' a quarter," the boy reported.

"That's fine," said the little man. "Our only difficulty now is that our stock's more than half gone. I must send a letter off to Philadelphia tonight. We can have more books shipped to Cincinnati and pick them up there."

Jonathan got a pen and paper and wrote the message as Mr. Greenfield dictated it. The letter was long, for it listed forty or fifty different titles. When it was finished, the boy sealed it with wax, wrote the address of the Philadelphia publisher on the outside, and carried it downtown to the post-office. The clerk weighed it.

"More'n half an ounce," he said. "That'll cost ye ten cents at the new low rates. I remember when a letter was forty cents to Philadelphy. Now it's only five cents a half-ounce fer three hundred mile. It'll git thar in a week or ten days, too. We shore live in an age o' speed an' progress!"

It was the first time in several days that Jonathan had been away from his employer's side for any length of time. He knew Mr. Greenfield was among friends at the boarding-house, and there was no reason for him to hurry back.

There was still light enough to see his way without difficulty as he turned toward the riverfront. He had an idea that he might find the Indiana-bound party of professors there, and have another chat with Noah Carter. Passing through a belt of warehouses and grog-shops, he came down to the docks. Three or four big, double-stacked river steam-ers were moored just below. The one nearest him had three decks and was fairly dripping with gingerbread work. It looked like a giant layer cake with white frosting.

None of the steamboats appeared to be near leaving. There was no smoke coming from their funnels and no crowd of passengers lining their rails. At this time of day, all activity seemed to have ceased along the waterfront, and the crews had gone up to the taverns. Jonathan went up to a surly-looking watchman who was leaning against one of the pilings and asked for news of the scholarly emigrants, but he got no answer except a mumbled oath or two.

He turned back and was on his way up a narrow street between two warehouses when he saw a man slip out of an alley ahead of him. In the dusk it was impossible to catch more than a shadowy glimpse of his face. But the tall, tight-coated figure and the wide-brimmed hat sent a sudden chill down Jonathan's spine.

The man didn't look back. He went rapidly up the street as if in a hurry to get somewhere—or away from somewhere.

Jonathan waited till he had rounded the corner and disappeared. Then he followed cautiously. When he reached the alley he was half afraid to look, but he forced himself to stop and peer into the half darkness.

There was something there—a shapeless bundle lying in the mud with one arm stretched out. The boy took a deep breath and stepped closer. It was a huge, fat man, coatless and disheveled. There was a bloody bruise on the side of his head but he was breathing heavily. A sickening reek of liquor came from him.

Jonathan waited to see no more. The man was alive and would return to consciousness sooner or later. Meanwhile, if anyone chanced to see him hanging about, he was almost sure to be suspected of the attack. He hurried back to the riverfront and took another road up the hill.

It was only when he was half a mile from the scene that he began to blame himself for a coward. Why, he asked himself bitterly, hadn't he followed the man he had seen coming out of the alley? If that man was McKee—and he felt surer of it every minute—all the more reason for trying to catch him red-handed in his latest crime. The truth, he realized, was that he was afraid of the red-haired robber.

Suddenly he remembered the little pistol in his pocket. Until now he had had no opportunity to examine it. The short, rounded grip felt comfortable to his hand as he hurried along. When he reached a stretch of road where there were no houses, he took the pistol out and tried aiming it. It wasn't much of a weapon, he decided—hardly more than a toy. But it was well made and beautifully finished. In the twilight he could still see well enough to pour in a charge of powder, tamp it with the tiny ramrod that fitted under the barrel, push a bullet into place with a paper patch, and lower the hammer carefully over a percussion cap.

Armed with a loaded pistol he looked over his shoulder defiantly, half hoping to find McKee following him. Lights twinkled in the town below him but there was nobody on the road. He put the little gun back in his pocket and returned to the boarding-house.

. . .

Mr. Greenfield, Jonathan found, was as eager to move on as he was himself. They could have sold all the remaining stock of books in Pittsburgh, but the little man preferred to dispense his wares in the country districts. "After all," he explained, "the people here can always get books from the local merchants or send East for them. It's folks on the backwoods farms who really need us."

They invested some of their cash in flour, bacon, and grain for the mare, and prepared to leave the morning of the third day.

There was a drizzle of warm rain falling when they drove down to the ferry. A good-sized crowd was gathered on the riverfront, and horses and wagons were being loaded on the lower deck of one of the steamboats.

"Wait a minute!" cried Jonathan. "That's the Carters. I want to say good-bye to Noah."

He pulled Dolly to the left, out of the way of traffic, and left the van there while he ran down the dock.

Noah greeted him warmly. "You heard why we didn't sail yesterday, I guess," he said. "The steamboat captain was knocked on the head and robbed night before last. He told the police he knew who it was and a gang of river men set out to try to catch him, but he got away. A fellow named McKee, they say. He seems to have quite a reputation as a highwayman in these parts. Ever hear of him?"

"Yes," said Jonathan soberly. "I've heard of him."

"Well, I understand the river shippers have gotten together five hundred dollars reward for him, dead or alive!"

The Massachusetts' lad's eyes shone as he announced this bit of news. "I tell you, Jonathan," he grinned, "we're really in the wild and woolly West!"

All the other passengers were aboard the steamer now. The boys shook hands and Noah started for the gangplank. "Don't forget to look us up in Bloomington," he called over his shoulder.

An hour later Jonathan drove old Dolly off the ferry and they started the fifty-mile journey overland to Steubenville.

The rain made reading impossible in the front seat, which had a canvas roof but was open on three sides. Mr. Greenfield refused to seek shelter inside. He was well wrapped in an old greatcoat that kept his plump body dry.

"I like this weather," he told Jonathan. "A summer rain brings out the smell of the earth and leaves and flowers.

Until you're blind, you don't notice such things, but they mean a great deal to me."

The country they traveled through that day was hilly and wild, with few homes or settlements. The rain stopped falling before dark, but Jonathan had a hard time finding wood dry enough for a supper fire. He slept under the wagon that night, wrapped in a stiff tarpaulin.

The next day was clear and cool. They made a good twenty-five miles and from the hill where they camped that evening they could see the Ohio and the distant spires of Steubenville on the farther bank.

When they reached the river in the morning the ferry-boat was on the other side and they had an hour's wait. It was nearing noon by the time they drove up from the water-front into the bustling Ohio town.

"I think you'll like this state," Mr. Greenfield told his young driver. "I've always felt a difference, once I got into Ohio. Folks came here to live, not just to make money. It's a settled, peaceful sort of country."

Jonathan thought Steubenville very little different from Pittsburgh and other river towns he had seen. But when they took the road again after dinner, he began to understand what the bookseller meant. The farms and the little villages were neat and well-ordered. The people were friendly and hospitable. Several housewives offered them generous refreshment in the form of strawberries and cream, rhubarb pie and other good things. And more than one farmer, busy with his haying, dropped his scythe or his fork to chat with them by the roadside.

They sold a dozen books before nightfall.

"These Ohio folks are great ones to read," the bookseller commented. "They set a lot of store by education. The state's pretty young yet, but they've already got seven or eight colleges and new ones popping up every year."

The days went by pleasantly as they journeyed southwestward. It was mid-June now, with corn nearly waist-high in the fields and leaves heavy on the trees. Jonathan read book after book as Dolly jogged along the country lanes. They passed through sleepy little towns, stopped for the night at prosperous farms, ate themselves fat and did such a business that the book-shelves in the wagon began to look bare.

Their route took them through Cambridge, then west to Zanesville and southwest again toward Lancaster. From there the road led almost straight to Cincinnati. Mr. Greenfield was anxious to reach the big town on the Ohio now. The books people asked for were nearly always out of stock, and the few volumes that remained were largely sermons and dry old works that nobody wanted.

"I hate to disappoint so many folks," he told Jonathan. "They deserve better stuff, when there are so many fine books in the world. It'll be the Fourth of July before you know it, and I figure my order will surely be in Cincinnati by then. Get up, Dolly! Move those lazy feet!"

Much as he was enjoying the trip, Jonathan, too, was eager to get there. He worried about the money that was accumulating in his employer's plump purse. The bookseller never thought of concealing his cash. When he made change for a customer, the big roll of bills and the clinking silver were there for anyone to see. The boy took some comfort from the feel of the pistol in his pocket, but he still slept lightly when they camped along the road.

The last Sunday in June found them in Pickaway County, two-thirds of the state behind them. The little bookseller made a point of doing no trading on the Sabbath. They hitched the mare in a long row of vehicles under the trees by a crossroads church and went in to join the congregation. Mr. Greenfield had insisted on buying Jonathan a new outfit of clothes the week before, so that the boy no longer needed to be ashamed of his appearance.

It was warm and drowsy in the church. The good farm people sang their hymns lustily and settled down for the sermon. Within five minutes Mr. Greenfield's head was nodding and he dropped off to sleep with a gentle smile on his round, pink face. Jonathan tried to listen to the droning words that came from the pulpit but his thoughts wandered. He was staring out the window at a pair of cardinals, vivid among the leaves of a horse-chestnut tree, when something the preacher said brought him back with a start.

"Sin," the man in the pulpit intoned, "has come to our midst. Black sin—the sin of robbery and murder. I say murder, for even now the pitiful victim lies at death's door. Our prayers should rise to Heaven that the life of that good woman, our long-time neighbor, be spared by a merciful Providence. And we should pray, too, that the foul fiend who laid her low be speedily apprehended and brought to the stern bar of justice."

There was a rustle of movement in the congregation. The men looked grim and the women were pale and disturbed. Boys and girls listened with eager interest. Only the little bookseller slept on, snoring very faintly.

Jonathan caught two or three faces turned in their direction and was startled to see a look of suspicion in the eyes of a boy who stared at him from the other side of the aisle. Did these people take his blind employer and himself for robbers? He squirmed in his seat and concentrated his attention on the sermon.

There were no more references to that particular crime. The minister went into a long catalog of less interesting sins—pridefulness, vainglory, stinginess, addiction to strong liquors, covetousness, sloth and the like. He went on for more than an hour, and housewives with dinners to get were beginning to get as fidgety as their children when the service ended.

Mr. Greenfield had wakened from his nap some moments earlier, and Jonathan was relieved when the preacher hurried down to greet him as an old acquaintance. While they were talking he turned to the boy who had sat across the aisle.

"We've been traveling," he explained, "and just got here before church. What's this about a robbery?"

"He was talkin' about the Widow Peters," said the other lad. "Lives a couple o' mile north o' here. Some time last night she got a crack on the head an' her money was stole."

"Do they know who did it?" Jonathan asked.

"Ain't sure. But the only stranger we've seen 'round here till you come was a red-headed feller ridin' a roan horse. That was yesterday, an' he's dropped out o' sight. So I reckon he's the one."

"Did you get a look at him—at the red-headed man—yourself?" asked Jonathan tensely.

"Nope. All I know is what folks say. Why—you think you know who it is?"

The Maine boy shook his head. "No," he said. "It couldn't be the same one—way out here."

# *TWELVE*

THEY WERE INVITED TO DINNER AT THE MINISTER'S HOUSE. The conversation was dull enough as far as Jonathan was concerned, for the older men got into a long discussion of Latin and Greek writers whose names and ideas meant little to him. He kept his ears sharp for any mention of the Widow Peters' affair but the subject wasn't brought up. About three o'clock the preacher yawned and announced that he needed his Sunday afternoon nap, so they were able to break away. Jonathan hitched up the mare and they took the road again.

The day was hot and sultry with a threat of thundershowers in the air. Mr. Greenfield dozed quietly on the wagon seat, and Jonathan felt his own eyelids droop from time to time as Dolly plodded westward.

His drowsiness was interrupted by a sudden thudding of hoofs on the road behind them. He peered back around the side of the van in alarm. Three men on heavy farm horses came pounding past in a great cloud of dust. Each carried a rifle or a shotgun and their faces were grim and scowling. The last of the trio turned in his saddle to shout at the boy.

"Seen a man on a roan horse?" he bellowed.

"No!" Jonathan yelled back, shaking his head.

The horsemen disappeared over the next rise and Mr. Greenfield woke up.

"Eh?" he said. "What was that? I must have been nodding and didn't catch your remark."

"I was just talking to some people going by," Jonathan explained. "Looks as if we'd get a storm before dark."

"Yes," the bookseller agreed. "I can feel it in the air. How late is it now, by the way?"

" 'Round five o'clock, I'd say. If it comes on to rain I'll look for a farmhouse where we can put up."

They drove on for another hour and the sky in the south-west began to blacken ominously. At the first rumble of thunder Mr. Greenfield gave an uneasy start.

"Any houses in sight?" he asked. "These Ohio gusts can be quite violent."

"No houses," Jonathan told him. "But there's an old hay-barn over yonder in a clearing at the edge o' the woods. We'll make for that."

He guided Dolly through a field full of sparse grass and half-rotted stumps. The barn was a ramshackle structure of weathered boards with a bark roof. It had a lonesome, deserted look. The wide doors sagged on thin strap hinges and swung crazily in the rising wind.

Jonathan jumped down and pulled the doors open just as the first big drops of rain drummed on the wagon top. Dolly hurried in without urging, anxious to get under shelter.

By such dim light as came in from outside the boy could see that the place was empty except for a hummock of old hay in one corner. It had no floor, but the wall timbers looked sound and fairly strong. There were a few chinks in the roof, through which rain had already begun to drip.

"It's not much good," he told his employer, "but I reckon it'll do. We'd better not build a fire in here. Can you make out with a cold supper?"

"Yes, indeed," said the bookseller. "After that big dinner

I could go without well enough. But we may as well have some bread and cheese."

Jonathan set the bucket out under the eaves to catch rain water and came back to unharness the mare. It was then that he noticed a depression in the earth near the wall. Bending down to see better, he found fresh hoof marks. Sometime within the past day or two, a horse had stood there and pawed the ground with shod forefeet.

When he had unhitched Dolly and given her grain, he took time for a more careful inspection of the place. But in the semi-darkness, broken only by occasional lightning flashes, he could find no further clues to the barn's recent occupant.

They munched their cold meal, washed it down with water from the bucket, and prepared for bed. Jonathan spread his blanket on the pile of hay in the corner. After a while the storm spent itself, rumbling away over the hills, and they went to sleep.

A meadowlark was singing in the fresh dawn when the boy woke. He felt stiff and there was a puzzling sore place on the back of his thigh. He got up and felt under the loose hay. There was something hard and bumpy there, and he pulled out an odd-shaped wooden rack, curved on one side and with a pair of leather straps fastened to its edge. It was about two feet square. As he handled it he was aware of a strong horsy smell. Somewhere he had seen a gadget like that, but for the moment he couldn't remember where or when.

At least the thing would serve as fuel for a breakfast fire. He carried some dry hay outside to use as tinder, got the ax from the wagon and was about to chop up the wooden frame when a sudden recollection stopped his lifted arm.

Tom Cole! That was it—when he showed Jonathan his paintings that night, he had lifted the case from just such a rack, buckled to two rings in the saddle cantle!

The boy stood there, ax in hand, staring at the contraption. It was impossible, he thought, that it could be the same rack he had seen on Cole's roan. Perhaps in this part of the country it was a common thing to carry a light load on the horse's rump, and this was one of many such contrivances.

In any case he needed firewood. He split the thing up, started a kettle of water boiling and called Mr. Greenfield. While the little man was preparing breakfast Jonathan went inside and took another look at the pawed earth by daylight. At one side there was one complete track that was fairly clear. It was made by a big, well-shaped hoof. The shoe had been worn smooth and its edges were rounded, but in its outer side near the toe there was a deep nick. He tried to picture the horse that had made the track, and found himself thinking of a roan—a big roan with a red-haired rider. He wondered if the three armed farmers had found the man they were hunting.

The book wagon was on the road again by seven, and at noon they reached Washington Court House.

"It seems very quiet here," Mr. Greenfield remarked as they drove up the main street. "I remember what a bustle the place was in last year. It's a county town and court was in session."

Jonathan, too, thought the street looked strangely deserted. The dust lay undisturbed under the shade trees, and there were no horses tied along the courthouse hitching rail.

At the tavern it was the proprietor's wife who served them dinner. She had a flustered look.

"Tom's gone off with all the other menfolks," she told them. "Sheriff got up a posse 'fore daylight this mornin', an' they rode off to look fer this robber feller. If you come over from Pickaway, you must ha' heard the rumpus there. They tell me he nigh killed the Widder Peters an' got off with her cash. Makes me skeered to look out in the yard fer fear I'll see him ridin' in here—an' not a man around to stop him!"

"Dear me!" exclaimed the bookseller in distress. "I hadn't heard a word about it. Strange, too, for I was at the pastor's house for dinner. But surely you needn't fear any open attack here in daylight!"

"I dunno," the woman fretted. "Seems like this man is

mighty bold. I've got the money an' the silver hid, but I ain't anxious to be knocked in the head like a steer."

By the time the "Athenaeum" was ready to depart, the sheriff's posse was beginning to straggle back into town. Glum-faced men got off their tired horses and came into the bar to wet down dusty throats. They had little to say beyond the fact that none of them had seen hide nor hair of their quarry.

"Prob'ly he's halfway to the Miami River by now," one grumpy citizen growled. "Must ha' rode all night to git sech a long start on us."

Mr. Greenfield was plainly troubled when they resumed their journey. It wasn't fear for himself, Jonathan saw, but unhappiness that such things should happen in peaceful Ohio.

"I wouldn't worry too much," he tried to reassure the little man. "This robber sounds to me like the same one that knocked out the steamboat captain in Pittsburgh. He was red-headed, too. So most likely he's a Pennsylvanian —one o' those rough customers from up the Monongahela."

"You think so?" asked the bookseller with relief. "I'd hate to believe these pleasant people about here had turned to banditry. It's queer, though, that I hadn't heard about the affair earlier."

Jonathan changed the subject. "It's a nice afternoon and a good road," he suggested. "An' we've still got part o' that book by Scott to finish. Want me to read a spell?"

Mr. Greenfield agreed with enthusiasm, and the rest of the day passed pleasantly. The country they passed through was peaceful enough. Jonathan didn't see a gun all afternoon, nor hear a horse galloping, though he kept his ears open. The farmers were working in their fields and the cattle and sheep grazed in rolling green pastures. A smell of good cooking drifted out from open kitchen doors.

They spent the night at one of those solid farmhouses in Clinton County, undisturbed by any news of robberies. And for the next two days, as they traveled down toward Cincinnati, the only talk they heard was of crops and politics.

It was the evening of the second of July when the wagon came over the crown of the bluff and the Ohio Valley lay spread out before them. Dolly leaned back in the breeching and Jonathan applied the foot brake, for the road was steep. The boy was amazed at the size of the city below. Only a little over half a century before, Mr. Greenfield told him, Cincinnati had been a boat-landing in a howling wilderness. Now it had nearly sixty thousand people.

"They're smart people, too," said the bookseller. "Good readers. The city has enough free schools for every child to get an education. Some day the whole nation may do as well, though I doubt if I'll live to see it."

At Jonathan's age, leadership in schools didn't seem

particularly interesting. What impressed him more was the prosperous look of the houses they passed. Many of them were stoutly built of red brick, newer and cleaner than those he had seen in New York and Baltimore, and with more ground around them.

Almost every house had its lawn and garden, and the scent of roses was heavy in the evening air.

"Turn right at the foot of the hill," said Mr. Greenfield, "and drive three blocks. Then ask somebody for Mrs. Becker's boarding-house. It's in that neighborhood."

A few minutes later Jonathan was directed to a large, comfortable-looking brick house on a shady side street. There was a stable at the rear where he unharnessed Dolly and turned her over to a shock-headed blond youth who introduced himself as Mrs. Becker's son, Ludwig.

They were late for the regular supper but the stout, smiling German woman who greeted them soon served up a bountiful meal in the kitchen. She was an old friend of the bookseller's and asked him many questions about his travels while they ate.

"You make a good, long stay here this time, eh?" she asked.

"That depends," the blind man told her. "I'm hoping a shipment of books has arrived from Philadelphia. If it's here we can go on in a couple of days. Otherwise we'll have to wait. And," he added gallantly, "I can think of no pleasanter place to do it."

Jonathan accompanied him down to the freight office on the riverfront early next morning. No boxes had come in for Mr. Greenfield, the clerk told them, but a steamboat—the *Shawnee Queen*—was expected down from Pittsburgh that afternoon, and she might have the shipment aboard.

They strolled along the clean, cobbled wharfside and watched the drays loading and unloading. A steamer was just in from Louisville and the Negro roustabouts were rolling barrels of molasses and tobacco and bales of cotton from her cargo deck to the pier.

They went up through the business district, and the bookseller suggested that Jonathan buy a newspaper. "We've been out of the current of events so long," he remarked, "that we need to brush up. A daily paper is a luxury I've missed."

Back at Mrs. Becker's, they sat in the comfortable rockers on her front porch and Jonathan read the news, column by column. National politics filled most of the first page. The doings of the Congress and of President Polk caused the little bookseller frequent clucks of distress.

"I had great hopes that we could elect Harry Clay last fall," he sighed. "A Whig administration might have kept us out of trouble. I don't trust Polk and these fire-eating Democrats. They'll have us at war with the Mexicans in another year."

Jonathan labored on through the local items, the dispatches from the state capital at Columbus, and reports of lawsuits and court decisions. He was well into the back pages and about to start on advertisements of steamboat sailings when his eye fell on a column headed "News from the Back Counties."

"A packet of news freshly arrived from Fayette and Pickaway Counties," he read, "contains the regrettable intelligence that a murderous robber has been conducting his nefarious practices in that area. On the 26th of June, Mrs. Peters, an elderly widow of Pickaway County, was beaten and robbed in her home, recovering her senses for only a few moments before her death on the 28th. An armed posse, summoned by Sheriff Bolton of Fayette, pursued the perpetrator of the felonious act without success. It is now believed that the bandit has headed north and may have taken to the woods. Mrs. Peters described him as a tall man with red hair, riding a roan horse. He was further described as having a scar at one side of the mouth. It is believed that the criminal may be the notorious McKee, wanted for several robberies in Pennsylvania."

Mr. Greenfield sat silent for a moment after the boy finished reading.

"Well, Jonathan," he said at length, "it seems your guess was pretty nearly right."

# THIRTEEN

THE "SHAWNEE QUEEN" MUST HAVE BEEN DELAYED SOMEwhere up the river, for she failed to put in an appearance that afternoon. Resigned to waiting, Jonathan spent the evening exploring the town and went to bed about nine-thirty.

At midnight he was awakened by a banging of guns and wild ringing of church bells. "Fire!" was his first thought, and he sprang out of bed in a panic. Then he heard a chuckle from his employer, who shared the room with him.

"Hurrah for the Glorious Fourth!" said Mr. Greenfield. "They make a real celebration of it here in the West."

Jonathan crawled back under the covers, but the din continued. Horns and steamboat whistles hooted, small boys yelled like Indians, and the bells and guns kept up their clamor for the better part of an hour.

At the first light of dawn the noise started again, and Jonathan got up and dressed. This, he decided, was the chance he had awaited to try shooting his pistol.

He tiptoed out and hurried up the hill to a wooded bluff where there were no houses. He took the little weapon from his pocket, set up a stick for a target and backed away five or six paces. When he pulled the trigger he half expected that nothing would happen. But the pistol went off with a smart, satisfying *bang* and jumped sharply in his hand. The stick target, to his amazement, fell over with a clean split through the middle.

"Gee!" the boy grinned to himself. "I must be considerable of a shot after all!"

He reloaded and fired several more times, with only fair success. That first shot had evidently been lucky. However, after half a dozen rounds he knew he could come within a foot of hitting what he aimed at. He cleaned the little gun, loaded it carefully and returned it to its hiding place.

Mr. Greenfield was up when he got back to the boarding-house, and the boy explained at breakfast that he had been out helping the town celebrate.

"We'll have to go down to the square when the public speaking starts," the bookseller told him. "There'll be some powerful oratory, I expect."

The day was clear and hot and soon the streets were filled with farm wagons and buggies, decorated with red, white and blue bunting. People were coming in from miles around to take part in the day's events.

By noon ten or twelve thousand perspiring citizens were packed in the principal square and a band on the flag-draped bandstand was pouring out such martial airs as "Yankee Doodle."

Lemonade booths were doing a rushing business and the many German settlers in the crowd were gathered around barrels of beer. There was little hard liquor in evidence, for Cincinnati was known as a temperance town. Throughout the proceedings nearly everybody in the throng remained orderly and good-natured.

After a deal of waiting, the mayor mounted the wooden rostrum, accompanied by a fat congressman who was to be the orator of the day. In spite of the July heat the lawmaker wore a black tail coat and a starched collar with points nearly up to his eyes. Following a lengthy and flowery introduction the orator poured himself a glass of ice water, quieted the lusty applause with an extended arm and began.

"Fellow citizens o' the great state of Ohio an' the Queen City o' the West," he boomed, "when I look into these noble and intelligent faces I hear the unfettered scream o' the American eagle . . ."

The eagle screamed quite a number of times in the next forty minutes, Jonathan thought. But the crowd loved it. They cheered every reference to "this great republic," "our peerless leaders" and "the glorious Acropolis of the West"—which, of course, was Cincinnati.

The boy watched the orator's collar wilt to a wrinkled rag and waited hopefully for the black coat to come off, but was disappointed.

The stout legislator was waving both arms and coming up to a thunderous climax when a gun barked sharply on the outskirts of the crowd. A few heads turned at the sound but most of the spectators took it for part of the celebration. Jonathan might have had the same idea if he had not caught sight of men running. There was a second shot, farther away this time, and then a faint sound of shouting voices.

Wedged in as he was, the boy had no chance to follow. He could only whisper in Mr. Greenfield's ear that he thought there was trouble back there.

The little man nodded. "I agree," he said. "Sounded to me as if somebody cried, 'Stop, thief!' But never mind—I want to hear the wind-up of this oration. The man's a second Demosthenes!"

His calmness made Jonathan feel a little foolish. He mopped his forehead and listened patiently to the final ringing words.

"What was he talking about?" he asked his employer when the roar of applause had subsided.

"Eh? Why, I don't know. But what a voice! A man who can tingle your spine like that doesn't need anything to talk about."

The crowd was beginning to break up, and Jonathan led the little bookseller out of the square toward the boarding-house.

At the first street-corner two small boys were talking excitedly. "I tell ya it *was* the police!" one of them insisted. "Look—there's the hole where the bullet hit—right under that store window!"

Jonathan stopped, staring at the splintered hole in the wall of the building. "What happened?" he asked the youngster. "Did you see it?"

"Sure, I did," the boy replied. "There was a feller in the edge o' the crowd—a red-headed feller in a broad-brim hat. Some farmer hollered out that he'd had his purse stole, an' this man started runnin'. They chased him an' the constable started shootin' at him, only he ducked up the street here an' I guess he got away."

Jonathan had little to say as they walked on. He was

thinking that red-headed robbers were getting mighty common in this part of the country.

Mrs. Becker was serving a late dinner for the benefit of boarders who had attended the speaking. Jonathan and his employer had just finished eating and stepped out on the porch when the long hoot of a steamboat whistle came from the riverfront. Smoke was rolling up from a pair of tall stacks that moved slowly westward along the wharf.

"It's a boat from up river," the boy exclaimed. "I wouldn't wonder if it's the *Shawnee Queen!*"

Mr. Greenfield put on his top hat and they hurried down to the wharf. The passengers had already left the boat and cargo was being carried ashore. For an hour the pair stood by, with Jonathan describing to his employer just what each item of freight looked like. At last he reported a big wooden box. Two sweating stevedores heaved it along the gangplank end over end, and when it finally came to rest Jonathan read the painted lettering—"Nathaniel Greenfield, Cincinnati, Ohio"—on its side.

The little bookseller patted the case fondly. "Fine," he said. "You go up and get Dolly and the wagon. I'll stay here with the books and pay the charges."

Jonathan drove the van down to the wharf and with the help of a pair of roustabouts they loaded the heavy box inside.

"There," said Mr. Greenfield happily, as they drove back

to the boarding-house, "we've got our new stock—enough to last out the trip—and there's still better than a hundred dollars left over. Here—you'd better count it and make sure I wasn't cheated."

Jonathan thumbed through the roll of bills in the purse. "That's right," he said. "A hundred an' twenty dollars. It's a lot o' money, Mr. Greenfield. Don't you think you'd better find a good place to hide it, somewhere in the wagon?"

But the little man gently pooh-poohed the idea. He had a childlike confidence in the goodness of the world, and the boy had to admit that it would take an exceptionally mean thief to molest such a friendly, peaceable soul.

Before suppertime they had uncrated the books and ranged them on the shelves of the van. Mr. Greenfield handled each volume lovingly, to "get the feel of it" as he explained. Jonathan read him the titles and he placed the books himself, so that he would be able to find them again.

That was their last night at Mrs. Becker's, and the motherly German woman filled them up with a mammoth supper of pig's knuckles and sauerkraut. Jonathan, not quite sure he liked the queer-tasting cabbage at first, ended by accepting a second helping.

In the morning they were up at sunrise and took a course northwestward out of the city.

"You're going to meet some Quakers, Jonathan," Mr.

FOR AN HOUR THE PAIR STOOD BY

Greenfield remarked as they walked up the steep bluff road beside the sweating mare. "This corner of Ohio and a lot of southern Indiana is a great place for Friends, as they'd rather be called."

"We've got quite a few back in Maine," the boy answered. "Uncle Eli says they're good people—the salt o' the earth."

The bookseller nodded. "I've known them all my life, around Philadelphia," said he, "and I'll agree with your uncle. A lot of the Friends here in the West came over the mountains from North Carolina about fifty years ago. Some of them had been wealthy planters and merchants and owned a good many slaves. But their consciences were troubled. They set a lot of store by conscience—what they call the inner light—the voice of God in their hearts. So when the Lord told them it was wrong to hold slaves, they freed them.

"Right away that got them into difficulties with their neighbors. And it didn't do the poor Negroes any good because as soon as they were freed the state passed a law that they could be picked up and sold right back into slavery.

"The Friends couldn't stand that, so they got rid of their houses and lands and moved over into free territory across the Ohio. They're peace-loving people, but they're stubborn, too. Nowadays when a slave runs away and heads north he's pretty sure to find a Quaker who's ready to help him escape, law or no law."

Jonathan had an opportunity to learn more about the Friends at first hand that evening. The van had covered twenty miles or more since they left Cincinnati, and they were close to the Indiana line when Mr. Greenfield suggested that they look for a place to spend the night.

A short distance ahead Jonathan could see a small farmhouse, new and freshly painted. A young man of twenty-two or -three was just crossing the road from the field where he had been shocking wheat. He was carrying the long scythe with its wooden cradle on his shoulder.

The farmer paused, read the sign on the wagon's side, and his sunburned face lighted up with a smile.

"I see thee's got books for sale," he called to Mr. Greenfield. "Won't thee stop in? My wife's quite a hand to read."

From the proud way he said "my wife" Jonathan was fairly sure he was a recent bridegroom.

"We'll be glad indeed to stop," the bookseller answered. "And if you can find room for us we'd like to pay for a night's lodging."

The young man flushed an even deeper red. "I'll have t-to speak to Sophia about that," he stammered. "But you folks drive right in anyway."

He hurried into the house and Jonathan headed Dolly toward the barn. Mr. Greenfield chuckled. "How old does our host look?" he asked. "Sounds to me as if he and his wife haven't had time to do much entertaining yet."

The pretty girl who came to the back door was certainly not more than two years older than Jonathan. She had on a big flower-dotted apron and she stood there smiling, far more at ease than her husband.

"Supper'll be ready in a few minutes," she said. "You can wash in that pan on the bench and I'll bring a clean towel. We've got a spare room and I'm sure you won't mind sleeping on brand-new sheets."

She looked more closely at the bookseller. "Oh," she said softly, "I didn't realize thee was— I'm so sorry!"

"Think nothing of it, ma'am," he replied. "Jonathan, here, is eyes for me. Nathaniel Greenfield, at your service."

"I'm very glad to meet thee," she said. "And thee, too, Jonathan. My name is Sophia Cope, and this is Amos Cope, my husband."

The young bride served them a very good meal. When it was over and the dishes were washed, she joined them in the tiny parlor.

"Now," she told the bookseller, "I want to hear about thy books."

Mr. Greenfield plunged at once into a conversation on the subject nearest his heart, and while they talked Jonathan got better acquainted with Amos Cope. He had come from Wilmington, Ohio, two years before, and started the farm, building a shack for himself and a lean-to for his oxen. When he had it cleared and plowed and had harvested his first good crop, he built the house and barn. Then he went back for the girl. They had been married by the Quaker ceremony in the meetinghouse at Wilmington, and that, he admitted with a grin, was only three months ago.

Mrs. Cope and her husband were both graduates of the Friends' Academy in their home town. They were intelligent, well-read young people and there were already a dozen or more volumes in their new parlor bookcase. That was a lot of books for a farm family in the West, but before the evening ended they bought two more—"Legends of New England," by the rising young Quaker poet, John G. Whittier, and a volume of Daniel Webster's speeches.

The travelers slept well that night in the spare room of the little house. Amos Cope was up long before them, doing his barn chores, and his wife had breakfast on the table by the time they were dressed. In spite of all Mr. Greenfield's efforts she refused to take any money for their entertainment.

"You've been our very first guests," she said. "I wouldn't feel right to be paid for that pleasure."

The bookseller finally accepted her refusal, but before they left he brought a copy of Cobbett's "The American Gardener" from the van and put it in her hands.

"I can smell your flowers," he said, "so I know you like

gardening. You'll find a good friend in William Cobbett."

It was hard to tear away from this pleasant homestead. The Copes walked hand in hand beside the wagon as far as the road.

"Be sure to visit us again if thee comes this way," the young farmer told Mr. Greenfield. "And I'd make a point of stopping at Sheldon's Grove when thee gets over into Indiana. There's a big settlement of Friends there and I know they'll want thy books. Look up Joel Benton—Dr. Joel Benton, the physician. He's college-educated and considerable of a reader."

Then the good-byes were said and they were on their way.

"As nice a young couple as ever started life together," the bookseller smiled, and Jonathan agreed with him.

They crossed the state line before noon and jogged on along fair country roads, stopping from time to time to peddle their literary wares. About sunset they came to a fork where a battered signpost stood.

"It says 'Sheldon's Grove, six miles,' " Jonathan told his employer. "Want to take that road? It'll be dark pretty soon."

"We'll go there in the morning," Mr. Greenfield decided. "Meanwhile, it feels like a good night to camp out. I've slept indoors so much lately I'm getting spoiled."

Jonathan drove along for a mile or two before he found

a good camping place. It was out of sight of any farmhouses, in a fine grove of butternuts, where the road forded a small stream. He guided Dolly in among the trees, unharnessed her and set about building a fire.

It was twilight and the whippoorwills were calling when he went down to the brook for water. But the sound he heard as he lifted the dripping bucket from the stream was not made by any bird. It was a muffled thump, followed by a kind of moaning sigh. The mare snorted loudly, as if in fear.

Quietly, Jonathan set down the pail and reached into his pocket. With the pistol in his hand he started running, light-footed, toward the campfire.

# *FOURTEEN*

IN THE DARKNESS THERE UNDER THE TREES IT WAS HARD TO see anything. Jonathan was within a dozen yards of the fire before he made out the crouching figure silhouetted against the blaze. It wasn't the plump little bookseller, he could tell at a glance. The man was big and angular and a drooping, broad-brimmed hat hid his face.

Then Jonathan saw what he was doing. Stretched on the ground was the body of Mr. Greenfield, and the stranger's hands were hastily searching his pockets. There was no fear in the boy's heart—only a cold, relentless anger. With a steady thumb he cocked the hammer of the pistol.

At the clicking sound the man jerked to his feet and turned, snatching at his belt. Jonathan saw metal glint in the firelight as the heavy horse pistol was pulled free, and the next instant there was a blinding flash and a crashing report that shook the boy to his boot soles. Then the man rushed him.

Jonathan didn't know whether he was hit or not. He raised his little weapon, aimed it and pulled the trigger, all in one quick motion. Three steps away his assailant stumbled. His body seemed to double up and he fell sprawling, almost at the boy's feet. The big pistol flew out of his hand, clattering on a root a yard away. Jonathan picked it up.

The man's hat had fallen off and his tangled hair glowed red in the light of the fire. He gave a groaning curse, pulled his arms under him and tried to push himself up. Still acting automatically, Jonathan swung the heavy pistol like a club and brought the butt down on the back of the intruder's head. After that he lay quiet.

The boy left him there and ran to his employer's side.

Mr. Greenfield lay as if dead. Blood trickled slowly from a great gash on his temple, staining his white hair with crimson. Trembling, Jonathan knelt and laid an ear to the old man's chest. He couldn't be sure, but he thought the heart was beating, very slow and faint.

The reaction had hit the boy now. He sat down shakily, trying to think what was best for him to do. After a moment it occurred to him that he ought to make sure the robber was properly secured. He went back to the red-haired man, seized him under the arms and dragged him close to the fire. There was no mistaking that long scar that twisted the left corner of the open mouth.

McKee was breathing heavily, though he was still unconscious. A bullet wound in his chest near the right shoulder was bleeding fast and the whole side of his shirt was red. Jonathan ran to the wagon for a piece of rope with which he tied the man's wrists behind him. Then he brought up the pail of water from the brook, washed Mr. Greenfield's wound and gave the mare a drink. There was no time to feed her, for he knew he must get the two wounded men to a doctor.

As he backed Dolly into the shafts she lifted her head and whinnied. An answering neigh came from the roadside. Jonathan marked its direction and as soon as he had fastened the traces he walked toward the sound. Tied to a tree at the edge of the grove he found the big roan horse he had expected.

The animal was uneasy, pawing and snorting as if it had caught the smell of trouble. When he patted its neck, the mane was matted and unkempt and he could feel the roughness of dried mud on the lean flanks. Gently he untied the reins from the tree and led the horse into the grove.

Jonathan added wood to the fire. When it blazed up he took a closer look at the tall roan, for there was something strangely familiar about its appearance. The boy's mind flashed back to the night on the mountain when Tom Cole had been their supper guest. Could he be mistaken? Hastily he passed his hand over the saddle. The silver studs and mountings were there, and under the cantle were the two metal rings he remembered. With a feeling of cold dread he wondered if the young painter lay murdered somewhere in the Pennsylvania hills.

But now there was no time to waste. He backed the wagon around and opened its rear door. Putting forth all his strength he lifted Mr. Greenfield and laid him on the neatly made bed inside. McKee, for all his height, was easier to handle. Jonathan hoisted him up and flung him like a sack of meal over the roan's saddle. The horse snorted and plunged but he was able to quiet him. He tied the reins to the back of the van, kicked dirt on the fire and led Dolly out to the road.

Jonathan tried to recall Amos Cope's parting words.

Something about a doctor in Sheldon's Grove. Dr. Joel—Burton? Belton? Benton—that was it! He slapped the mare's rump with the ends of the reins and urged her out of her slow trot into a lumbering gallop.

"I hate to do it, old lady," he told the tired animal, "but this is mighty serious business."

That ride seemed to Jonathan to drag on endlessly. Actually it was not more than half an hour before he saw the scattered lights of a village ahead. As they entered the main street he eased the lathered mare down to a walk, and at the first house that showed a light in the window, he jumped down and rapped at the door.

"Can you tell me where the doctor lives—Dr. Benton?" he asked the elderly woman who answered his knock.

"Yes, Friend," she said. "It's the big white house yonder—third on the left. If thee's hurt or in trouble I'd be glad to help—"

"Thanks," he nodded hastily, and ran back to the wagon.

At the door of the white house he knocked again. A girl opened it and stood staring at his face, white and strained in the lamplight.

"Is the doctor here?" he panted.

"Yes," she said. "Won't thee come in?"

"I've got two men out there at the wagon," he told her. "Both of 'em may be dying. Could the doctor come out?"

"I'll get him," said the girl. "Thee drive in here beside

the house and he'll be right out."

By the time Jonathan brought the van into the dooryard, he found a tall, vigorous-looking, gray-haired man standing there in his shirt-sleeves. The doctor wasted no time in questions, but lifted McKee's limp body off the saddle and took him inside. He returned at once to help Jonathan carry the little bookseller into the plainly furnished room that served as an office and lay him on a couch.

With quick, skillful fingers, the physician examined the gash on the old man's head. Then he turned to the red-haired robber, who was stretched out on the bare table.

"This one will surely bleed to death if we don't staunch that wound," he said. "The other may be in worse shape, but there's no immediate danger."

He ripped away McKee's shirt, washed the bullet-hole and stuffed it with clean lint. Then he bandaged his shoulder tightly with a long roll of cloth taken from the closet.

"I–I had to hit him on the head, too," said Jonathan. "That's what knocked him out."

"Nothing serious there," Dr. Benton reported. "I take it thee'd like to leave his hands tied. Is that right?"

"Yes," said Jonathan. "He tried to rob us. While I was off getting water he clubbed Mr. Greenfield on the head. Then he fired his pistol at me and missed. He'd have killed me if I hadn't shot him."

The doctor looked at him kindly. "I'm sorry thee had

to do it," he said, "but I can see how it was. Now let's look at thy friend."

The examination was a long one, for the physician had to proceed delicately. He did not speak until he stood up.

"There's a pretty severe fracture of the skull," he said, and his face was grave. "But the old gentleman's pulse is steady and he seems to have a strong constitution. If he pulls through tonight I think he may recover. Tell me, is he blind?"

"Yes," said Jonathan. "That's why he needed me to drive and do for him."

"Thee sounds like a Yankee," Dr. Benton remarked with a twinkle in his eye.

"I'm from Maine," the boy nodded. "I'm on my way west to my father's place in Illinois."

He hesitated. "There's just one thing," he said. "Before that robber comes to, I wish you'd search him. Mr. Greenfield had a wallet with more than a hundred dollars in it, and it seems to be gone. You might see if he's got on a money-belt, too—a buckskin bag sewed onto an old harness strap. If he has, it's mine. It's a long story, but he stole it from me back in New York six or seven weeks ago."

The doctor produced the wallet. Then he felt under the waist of the robber's tight-fitting breeches and in a moment pulled forth the belt and pouch that Jonathan remembered so well.

"How much did thee have in it?" he asked.

"Close on to five hundred dollars, mostly in big bills—twenties an' fifties. An' say—" he remembered—"there was a letter from my father to my Uncle Eli Brent. Only I s'pose he'd have thrown that away."

"No," said Dr. Benton. "It's here. And three hundred—three-fifty—three hundred and ninety dollars. I know thee's telling the truth but we'll have to let the sheriff decide. Now, young man, thee looks a little pale. I don't suppose thee had any supper? Well, we'll take care of that."

He went into the next room. "Samantha," he called, "set out some food for our guest."

The same girl who had opened the door when he knocked now appeared from the kitchen, carrying bread and butter, cold meat and a jug of milk. She set them on the dining room table and smiled at Jonathan.

"After all thee's been through," she said, "I suppose thee hasn't much appetite. Thee really ought to eat something, though."

He found the first few mouthfuls hard to swallow, but soon discovered he was hungrier than he had thought. As he was drinking the last of the milk there was a sound of buggy wheels in the yard.

"That's likely Sheriff Evans," said the girl. "Father sent young Joel to fetch him."

The sheriff was a raw-boned man with drooping gray

mustaches. First he questioned the doctor, then asked Jonathan to tell his story. It was a slow business, for the law officer had to set down all the facts in a laborious hand.

"Well," said the sheriff, at last, "looks like ye can identify this McKee pretty positive. Th' authorities over in Ohio are lookin' for him—got the handbills today. An' ye say there's a reward offered in Pennsylvany. Take it all in all, seems like ye'd made quite a haul when ye lugged him in. I'll git my letters writ to Pittsburgh an' Pickaway County an' send 'em off tomorrer. An' long as the doc, here, says this scamp ain't goin' to die, I'll lodge him snug over at the jail. Here's yer money, son."

He handed Jonathan the money-belt.

Dr. Benton had been bandaging the bookseller's head during their conversation. Now he came over and laid a hand on Jonathan's shoulder.

"Sheriff," he said, "I think thee'll agree the county owes this lad something. No telling who might have been robbed and maybe killed if McKee hadn't been caught. Now thee doesn't want to have the expense of feeding and stabling that roan horse, does thee?"

"No," the officer replied. "Fer a fact, I don't. But I can see what ye're gettin' at, Doc. Think it'd be legal?"

"We're pretty sure the horse was stolen," said the doctor. "The boy is the only one who knows the owner. Why not put the horse in his custody, to return it when he can. I'll go his bond, if thee likes."

"Shucks," grinned the sheriff. "Don't need no bond. It's a deal, Doc. Here, I'll write out the paper now."

He took his pen and traced the words heavily, signing with a flourish at the bottom of the sheet. Then he handed it to Jonathan.

"Know all men by these presents," the boy read. "Remanded to the custiddy of the bearer, Jonathan Brent, this sixth day of July, 1845, in the County of Harley, State of Indiana, one Roan Horse, stole by one McKee from one Thos. Cole & to be reterned by said Jonathan Brent to said Cole as & when opertunity offers. Signed, Jacob Evans, Sheriff of Harley County."

"Gosh!" was all the boy could manage to gasp.

He shook hands, first with the sheriff, then with the smiling doctor.

It was about this time that the prisoner on the table gave a groan and opened his eyes. Before they could reach him he lurched to a sitting position, swung his feet to the floor and stood there swaying weakly while he glared around the room.

"Steady now, me bucko," said the sheriff, crowding McKee back against the table. "Try anything rough an' ye'll bust that wound open an' bleed to death. We'll jest take ye out to the buggy now an' put ye in a good safe place."

He propelled the red-haired man out the office door and hoisted him to the seat of the waiting vehicle.

"Leave yer address in Illinois with the doctor," he called over his shoulder to Jonathan. "If I git word about that reward I'll wanta write to ye."

"Well," said Dr. Benton, when the sheriff had gone, "it's fortunate I've got a good big barn. Thee'll find room for the 'Traveling Athenaeum' and stalls for the horses. I must go back to my patient."

Jonathan drove the wagon into the barn-floor and unhitched old Dolly and the roan. He watered them, gave them grain from the wagon-box and hay from the doctor's mow. Then, by the light of a lantern, he rubbed the flecks of dried lather off the mare's gray sides and curried the big saddle horse.

The roan was hollow-flanked and lean from overwork, but his hoofs and legs were sound and he ate with hearty appetite. Just for curiosity Jonathan lifted the forefeet and looked at the shoes. The iron was worn smooth and rounded, but in the edge of the off plate was a deep nick. He was certain now that one of those shoes had made the track he had seen in the old barn, back in Ohio.

The boy stood back and looked at the horse with admiration. "We've got to give you a name," he said. "Wish I knew what Tom Cole used to call you. Let's see—hmm—

Prince? No, that's too common. Roamer? Ranger? Hey—I know! I'll call you Doctor. If it hadn't been for Doc Benton I'd never have had you to ride. Now if only Mr. Greenfield pulls through safe—well—you and I'll make the dust fly on the road to Illinois."

# FIFTEEN

JONATHAN SHARED AN ATTIC BEDROOM WITH THE DOCTOR'S twelve-year-old son, Joel, that night. In the morning the boys came down for an early breakfast and heard encouraging news.

"The old gentleman recovered consciousness a little while ago," Dr. Benton told Jonathan. "He asked for thee and I told him thee was safe. That seemed to please him. His pulse is stronger and he's resting easily. Later, perhaps, it would help if thee went in and said a few words to him."

Mr. Greenfield had been moved to a bed in the guest room so that the doctor could use his office. He was busy with patients for the first hour or two after breakfast, then drove off behind his fast pacing mare to make some calls at outlying farms.

Jonathan spent the morning with Joel and Samantha. By noon they knew the whole history of his journey and had told him many things about Sheldon's Grove. He had begun to think of it as one of the most peaceful little places in the world when Joel gave his sister a questioning look, got a nod in return, and proceeded to tell him something that changed his ideas.

"It's a secret," the young Quaker said in a low voice. "We know thee can be trusted or we wouldn't tell thee. Right within two miles of here there's a station on the Underground."

"The Underground?" Jonathan asked, perplexed.

"Yes—the Underground Railway—to help runaway slaves. Hasn't thee ever heard of it? Slave-hunters from Kentucky come through our town often, but they haven't caught one yet. I reckon Sheriff Evans knows all about it. He stands by the folks around here, even if he isn't a Friend himself."

"How does it work?" asked the Maine boy.

"Well, suppose a Negro gets in trouble with his master,

or finds out he's going to be sold down the river. He runs away—hides in the woods and travels at night. If he can get to the Ohio he tries to swim across, or maybe he's carried over by someone in a boat. All the time the slave-catchers are hot after him. And just because he gets to Indiana it doesn't mean he's safe. The law is that they can come over here and catch him. The Underground is a chain of stations that reaches clear up to Michigan and over to Canada. Maybe a station is a farm, or a store or a house in some village. Each one hides the slave and feeds him and then passes him on to the next stop. How they do it is a secret—I guess they've got lots of ways."

"Father sometimes has to go out in the middle of the night," said Samantha, taking up the tale. "He doesn't talk about it, but we know there are Negroes who've been shot, or bitten by dogs, and need a doctor."

"Gosh!" said Jonathan. He looked at the two young Quakers with a new respect.

The doctor was late for the midday meal. He tied his mare in the dooryard and paid a hurried visit to the book-seller's room before he sat down at the table. Jonathan watched his expression anxiously and was relieved to see him smile.

"Thy friend is sleeping like a kitten," he told the boy. "I think he may be able to take some nourishment when he wakes, but I don't want to disturb him yet. Thee might have a little hot broth ready, Samantha—say about four o'clock."

Dr. Benton had other calls to make after dinner but he returned in mid-afternoon. He opened the door of the guest room gently, then beckoned to Jonathan. The boy tiptoed up the stairs and entered the darkened chamber. Mr. Greenfield stirred a little in the bed. His face looked pale and drawn beneath the big white bandage.

"Is that you, Jonathan?" he asked in a weak voice.

"Yes," said the boy, drawing close to the bed. "I—I hope you're feeling better, Mr. Greenfield."

"Just a headache," the old man answered slowly. "I tried—to warn you, son. The footstep didn't sound right. But—before I could shout—something hit me."

His voice trailed off, then became stronger as he continued.

"The books?" he asked. "The books are safe? And old Dolly? She's been pulling me around for nearly twenty years."

"All safe and sound," said Jonathan, trying to keep the choke out of his throat. "We even got the money back. And McKee's safe in jail."

The bookseller sighed a little and almost smiled. "That's good," he murmured. "Good."

The doctor laid his strong hand over his patient's. "I

think thee could have a little food now," he said. "Thee's come along splendidly so far, but some broth will do thee good."

At that moment Samantha appeared with a bowl and spoon, and Jonathan slipped out of the room. He was waiting in the office when Dr. Benton came down.

"Thee can stop worrying," the doctor said. "I'll tell thee honestly that I think he's going to get well. It may be several weeks before he'll be ready to travel again, but we'll take good care of him. I see no reason why thee shouldn't go on to thy father."

"I'd like to," said Jonathan. "Only—I don't want to leave him without a driver or anybody to help him on the road."

"That's something I've already thought of," replied the doctor. "There's a good, dependable farm boy, down the road a piece, who'll take over thy duties. I think thee can go with a clear conscience."

That evening Jonathan penned a letter to Tom Cole, in care of the Knickerbocker Club in New York. He gave a brief account of what had happened, and explained that he would make any arrangements about the return of the horse which the painter might suggest.

"I hope I never have to shoot a man again," he wrote in conclusion, "but the little pistol you left me sure came in handy. I want to give it back some day. You can reach me by writing to Matthew Brent's farm, near Blue Prairie, in Wales County, Illinois."

. . .

At eight o'clock of a fine, sunny July morning, Jonathan rode westward out of Sheldon's Grove on his way across Indiana. Taking leave of Dr. Benton and his family had been like parting with old friends, but there was no one in whose care he would rather leave Mr. Greenfield. Now that the old man was definitely improving, Jonathan was eager to finish his journey. He thought his father must have expected him weeks earlier and might now be worried about him.

The big roan tossed his head and broke into an easy canter, as if he, too, wanted action. Well-fed and rested, his flanks had filled out and his strawberry-speckled coat gleamed from the boy's brushing.

Jonathan had bought a canvas saddlebag from the harness maker in Sheldon's Grove and in it he carried such few spare clothes as he owned, a small pot and skillet, and some flour, tea and bacon. His blanket was rolled and tied behind the saddle, on top of a sack of oats.

The corn was tall in the fields now—a rustling green forest on either side of the road. It was amazing how the miles slipped past. Used to making twenty miles in a day behind the plodding mare, the boy found he had traveled farther than that before noon. He rested Doctor for an hour in the shade of a grove of trees and ate a lunch of biscuits and jam that Samantha had wrapped for him that morning.

When he mounted again he let the horse pick his own gait. Doctor was an excellent traveler. His steady lope was easy on the rider, but what was more important in covering distance was the fact that he was a naturally fast walker. Up hill and down he averaged six or seven miles an hour and never seemed to tire.

Jonathan rode through Shelbyville in the late afternoon and pushed on to the west. The weather was clear and hot and he wanted to camp in the open rather than spend the night at a tavern. It was growing dusk when he stopped at a Quaker farmhouse, bought a pint of milk and half a dozen eggs, and asked permission to sleep in the apple orchard, a short distance beyond.

He found a comfortable spot under the spreading branches of a big apple tree. Doctor was unsaddled, watered and fed, and tied to another tree close by. As he built his little cook-fire the boy realized for the first time how much he missed the companionship of the old bookseller. He was lonesome there by himself.

When darkness deepened, a hoot owl began calling, and its shivery cry set Jonathan's nerves on edge. He finished his supper, spread his blanket and lay down. All around him were small night noises—the monotonous chirp of crickets and the rustle of mice in the grass. He tried to sleep but his senses had never been more alert.

Perhaps an hour had passed when he heard a twig snap faintly, off to his left. The boy lay perfectly still, listening and staring into the dark. A long minute went by. Then a stick dropped among the embers of the fire and sent up a momentary flame. In that brief illumination he caught the glow of a pair of eyes, close to the ground and not more than ten paces away. "A dog," he thought.

Jonathan sprang to his feet and made a threatening gesture toward the creature crouching there. "Get out!" he shouted. "Go on home!"

He kicked the fire into a fresh blaze and picked up a burning brand. To his astonishment a big, dark figure rose slowly at the edge of the circle of light. A slurring, husky voice spoke.

"Don' drive me off, young marse. Ah's hongry an' Ah's hurted."

Shakily, step by step, a tall scarecrow of a man came toward the fire. When he was two or three yards away he sank down on his knees. His black body was bare to the waist and trickles of sweat ran down his pain-twisted face.

Jonathan found his voice at last. "You said you were hurt?"

"Hit's buckshot," the Negro mumbled. "In mah laig."

"I'll give you something to eat," said the boy, "and fix up

your wound the best I can. Are they pretty close—the folks that are after you?"

"Ah dunno, marse. Ah jes' kep' a-goin' arter Ah cross de ribber. Now Ah's almos' done."

"Well, crawl back there out o' the light while I build up the fire."

Fortunately Jonathan had three eggs left from his supper, and some bacon. While they fried in the pan he hurried down to the branch for water, and soon had tea brewing. When the meal was ready the runaway accepted it with a kind of dumb, unbelieving gratitude that touched the boy more than words.

"Now let's look at that leg," said Jonathan.

He washed the swollen, angry wound with hot water and tore up his second-best shirt to make a bandage.

"I guess you'll need a doctor," he told the big black. "I'm no hand at this sort of thing, but maybe it won't bleed as much now, and you'll be able to get some real help. Just wait here and I'll see what I can do."

He went back afoot to the farmhouse, wondering if the desperate Negro would steal his horse while he was gone. That was a chance he had to take.

There were no lights in the house, but the farmer thrust his head out a window in response to Jonathan's loud knocking.

"Yes?" he said sleepily. "What's troublin' thee, friend?"

"I'm the boy you let sleep in the orchard," said Jonathan. "There's a colored man up there—a runaway slave, with a bad leg wound. I don't know your politics, but I wondered if you'd be willing to help."

The man's head disappeared and in two or three minutes he came out the door, hitching up his galluses. "I'll fetch the rig," was all he said.

The boy rode with him back to the orchard. The fire had died down to a bed of red coals but everything else was as Jonathan had left it. Doctor scrambled up and snorted at the approach of the other horse, and the Negro sat staring, half afraid.

"It's all right," Jonathan told him. "This man's a Quaker. He'll take you to folks who'll help you."

He glanced at the farmer for corroboration and got a sober nod in reply. Together they helped the crippled man into the wagon and threw a heap of old grain bags over him.

As the white man climbed back to the wagon seat he turned to Jonathan. "I ain't mixed up in such things much," he said, "but I can't stand to see any human bein' suffer. I'll git him to the 'Railroad.' "

The wagon moved off between the rows of trees, then turned at the road and Jonathan heard the wheels rattling back toward the farmhouse. He went over and patted Doctor's sleek neck.

"Excitement's all over," he yawned. "Let's go back to bed."

He lay down once more, and this time neither hoot owls nor crickets could keep him awake. When next he opened his eyes, bright morning sunshine was glinting through the apple tree leaves.

He had made only two or three miles on the road to Franklin when two men on lathered horses overtook him. They reined in alongside the roan and one of them gave him a hard scrutiny.

"I'm the United States Marshal," the fellow announced, pointing to his badge. "We're after a runaway slave—big buck answerin' to the name o' Jethro. Prob'ly walks with a limp. You seen him?"

Jonathan considered a moment. "Yes," he said, "I guess I saw him last night."

"Where'bouts?"

"Back a piece—somewhere this side o' Shelbyville."

"Which way was he headed?" asked the marshal with quickened interest.

"The last I saw of him," the boy replied truthfully, "he was headed west."

"Good 'nough," grunted the officer. "Come on, mister, he can't have got far with that leg." And they spurred their horses into a gallop again.

It was two hours later, and more than a dozen miles

along the road, that Jonathan met the same pair returning. Their nags looked spent and the men were sour-faced. They eyed him somewhat resentfully, but said nothing as they rode past. When they were out of earshot the boy broke into a cheerful whistle. He had a feeling that Dr. Benton would have approved of his action.

# SIXTEEN

JONATHAN SLEPT NEAR MARTINSVILLE THAT NIGHT, AND pushed on westward the next day. He was anxious to reach the Wabash and get over into Illinois. Doctor had been doing forty-five or fifty miles a day and thriving on it, but now the weather turned hot and sultry and the boy held the pace down. It was real corn weather. Evening thunder-showers and blazing sun through the daylight hours pushed the green stalks skyward.

He reached the old river town of Terre Haute in the middle of a broiling afternoon and put up the roan at a livery stable. Then he went around to the courthouse to get some information about his route.

Flies buzzed in the dusty building and there was no sound of voices, for court was not in session. Jonathan picked his way along a tobacco-stained corridor and found an old man drowsing in a chair in the recorder's office. While he was hesitating as to whether he should wake him, a huge bluebottle fly settled on the bald head of the sleeper and he bounced up with a snort.

"Eh?" he asked, focusing his watery eyes on the boy. "What say, sonny?"

"I didn't say anything yet," said Jonathan. "But maybe you can help me if you've got any maps here. I'm trying to find my way to Wales County, over in Illinois."

The old man fussed about with the drawer of a big desk and finally pulled out a rolled-up parchment.

"Here we be," he announced in triumph, flattening out the map. "Wales County. Lies pretty nigh due west—'bout fifty or sixty mile. What place ye aimin' fer?"

"Blue Prairie," Jonathan told him, and they located a dot by that name on the map.

"All right, reckon ye kin find her now," said the old man. "Homesteadin'?"

The boy explained that his father had settled there.

"Well," remarked the county official, spitting in the direction of the brass cuspidor, "ever'body to his taste. Us

Hoosiers call Illinois folks 'Suckers,' 'cause they don't know enough to stay in Indianny. Still, there might be some fair to middlin' farmland out there."

Jonathan smiled as he left the courthouse. He had heard similar disparaging remarks about Indiana when he was in Ohio. He walked down to the bank of the Wabash and watched two or three fishermen angling for catfish. Then the sky began to darken and an afternoon shower came, breaking the heat and sending him back to his boardinghouse.

He got an early start next morning, in order to cover as much distance as possible in the cool of the day. An hour or two after he crossed the Wabash he came to a crude wooden marker by the roadside that told him he had reached the state line. Ahead of him was Illinois.

All the way west he had been wondering what the prairie would look like. But for the first few miles, at least, the country he traveled through was disappointingly like what he had left—rolling farms dotted with groves and rough, untidy stretches of woods.

The clearings and the houses seemed to grow smaller and fewer as he advanced. Along toward evening he rode over a low hill and reined Doctor in with a jerk. Ahead of him to the north and west was an immensity of gray-green space that took his breath away. Not a tree broke the vast emptiness that flowed to the horizon.

A mile or two away he saw a sod house and a low barn, so tiny in all that billowing sea of grass that they only seemed to emphasize its loneliness. He scanned the wide horizon eagerly, thinking he might find a herd of buffalo, but nothing moved as far as the eye could see.

Before it grew dark he came to a small stream and made camp there. The horse found plenty of forage on the grassy plain, and Jonathan himself was content to lie in his blanket, staring up at the stars. A few mosquitoes hummed about his head, but it was the thought of meeting his father that kept him awake.

Tomorrow he would see him for the first time in a dozen years. He had only a dim memory of a handsome, restless man with a curly brown beard—a man who had patted him on the head, told him to be a good boy at Uncle Eli's, and gone gaily away. "I'll come back for you when I've made my fortune," he had said.

Matthew Brent had never made a fortune. But perhaps, thought his son, he had settled down. Perhaps, with a new wife and a good, strong lad to help him, he would put down roots in this raw prairie land and make a living and a home.

After a long time the boy fell asleep, and the sun was already an hour high when he woke next morning. He made a hasty breakfast, washed, combed his hair and tried to brush his clothes into some semblance of neatness.

The road he followed was little more than a rutted track through the grass. Quail called far and near, and once a covey of prairie chickens went up with a roar of wings almost under Doctor's hoofs. After a few miles more farms began to appear. Whole sections of black earth had been plowed up and planted to corn that was now tall and well tasseled.

Jonathan turned in at a neatly painted frame house and asked the farmer how far it was to Blue Prairie.

"Not more'n ten or twelve mile," the man told him. " 'Tain't on this road, though. Lays over thataway—to the north. Ye'll see a trail to yer right, couple o' mile up the road. Foller that. Whose place ye lookin' fer?"

"Matthew Brent's," said Jonathan.

The farmer shook his head. "Thought I knew ever'body over there, but I ain't heard of him."

The boy found the trail leading northward a few minutes later and swung into it. The heat had become oppressive again as the day advanced, and he let Doctor follow the narrow track at a walk. There was still no sign of a town ahead when noontime arrived. Jonathan looked around for a place to rest, and for the first time he realized what it must be like to live in a country where there was no shade.

After another hot mile or two they came to a swale where water moved slowly among the reeds. Jonathan let the horse drink and nibble a few mouthfuls of grass before they went on. The redwing blackbirds that had been disturbed by their intrusion circled overhead and flew chattering back to the waterside.

The boy's heart began to beat faster when at last he sighted a cluster of buildings ahead. Blue Prairie turned out to be half a dozen frame houses—the kind of settlement they spoke of as "a wide place in the road," back home in Maine. There was a sleepy-looking general store, a blacksmith shop, a tiny, unpainted church and a one-room schoolhouse. The whole place had a wilted, deserted appearance in the shimmering heat.

Jonathan dismounted and threw the reins over a hitching-post. Two hound dogs lay sprawled on the sagging platform in front of the store. He stepped over and around them and went in through the open door. The dark interior was musty with the smell of such assorted articles as harness, salt pork, cheese and corn whisky.

A seedy-looking countryman was tilted back in a chair against the counter, chewing tobacco and making languid gestures at the swarm of flies that hung about his head. He stared vacantly at Jonathan.

"Are you the proprietor?" asked the boy.

The man seemed to meditate. "Nope," he said finally. "Reckon ye mean the storekeeper. He's in the back room havin' his chill."

"Maybe you can tell me how to find Matthew Brent's place," Jonathan suggested.

"Hm-m," said the man. "Brent. Seems like I've heered the name. Settled out towards the South Fork las' winter. Yeah—Matt Brent—he was the one. Take the wagon-trail out past the blacksmith shop an' go 'bout three mile. Ain't no other house near there."

Jonathan thanked him and went out. He wondered about the storekeeper. In that scorching heat it was hard to imagine having a chill, but he had heard about the fever and ague that afflicted so many settlers in this western country.

Now that he was so near the end of his long journey, the boy felt a mounting excitement in his veins. He had no idea how his father would receive him and he rather dreaded the meeting with his new stepmother, but he wanted to get the business over. That was why he urged the big roan to a gallop as they went down the prairie trail.

When he was still a mile away he saw the low, dark shape of a house above the sea of grass, and his eyes never left it during the long minutes that followed. As he drew nearer he could see that the building was no sod hut but a frame house, its roof still unfinished. Behind it a dozen acres had been plowed and there was straggly-looking corn growing there, the rows choked with high grass. That was strange, he thought. No hoeing had been done since the corn was planted.

The house stood stark and forlorn, the oiled paper that had been used instead of glass in its window frames hanging in tatters. A flower bed by the doorstep was grown up to weeds.

Jonathan swung down from his horse with a heavy feeling inside him. Something was wrong here. He went to the half-open door and knocked, and the sound echoed emptily in the afternoon heat.

When he got no answer he pushed the door wide and entered. Dust lay on the bare floors of the three small rooms. There was no furniture—not even a bedstead. In one corner of the kitchen, near the clay chimney, a pile of rags and prairie hay appeared to have been used as a sleeping place.

Jonathan's knees felt weak as he turned and hurried out. It was all like a bad dream. He wanted to wake up and find it wasn't true.

After a moment's hesitation he walked around to the back of the house. There was a thatched lean-to where a horse had been stabled. A plow with a rusty moldboard lay close by, and a crude well had been dug a few yards away. One other thing caught the boy's eye. It was a tiny patch of ground, fenced with sticks. Inside the fence there was newly turned earth, on which the grass was beginning to grow. And at one end of the heap of earth a white-painted pine board stood upright, glaring in the light of the setting sun.

Jonathan approached it with dragging feet. Even before he was close enough to read the roughly cut inscription on the board, he seemed to know what its message would be. But he forced himself to spell out the words, slowly and carefully—"Matthew Brent, born 1803, died June 12, 1845."

The boy's eyes were misty as he turned away, and his heart felt like a lump of lead under his ribs. He did not know how long he had been standing there when he heard somebody ride into the dooryard. A lop-eared mule appeared around the corner of the house. Perched on its bony back was an elderly Negro, gray and bent.

The old man climbed down stiffly and came toward Jonathan, a troubled look on his wrinkled face.

"You's Marse Matt's boy," he said softly. "He was lookin' fo' you all dem las' days."

Jonathan nodded, unable to speak.

"Too bad fo' you tó fin' de grave disaway, widout no foretellin'," the old colored man continued. "Marse Matt, he died las' mont' lak it say dar. Wukkin' on the roof o' de house, he was. Fell off an' bruk his neck. Ah done buried him an' de missus she tell me what to cyarve on de bo'd."

"You—you were working for him?" the boy asked.

"Yassuh. Ah's a free man—wukkin' fo' wages. Uncle Ned, dey calls me roun' yeah. Ah got no place else to go, so Ah done stay on."

"And Mrs. Brent?" asked Jonathan. "Where is she?"

"Dat Ah don' know, young Marse. She done lef' wid de fu'niture arter de buryin'. We-all spec somep'n musta happen to you, when de weeks went by. Marse Matt, he figger dey wouldn' let you leave whar you was at."

"No," said the boy heavily. "I left all right. Had some trouble along the way that held me up. I wish now—but never mind."

He sat down on the doorsill and stared at the wilted flowers in the tiny garden plot.

"My father had really started to make a farm here," he mused.

"Yassuh," said the old darky. "He done paid fo' it—a hull half-section. We got some plowin' done an' some co'n put in. But Ah took sick wid de misery, 'long in May, so de hoein' sorta got behin'."

Jonathan looked at the sky. "It's near sunset," he said. "I'll stay here tonight an' decide what to do in the morning."

Uncle Ned nodded and grinned. "Dat's fine, young Marse," said he. "Ah'll fix up some roas' yams an' hoecake fo' yo' supper. Reckon yo' hoss won' run off ef Ah tu'n him loose to pasture?"

"No," the boy replied. "He'll be all right. Give me a call when supper's ready. I think maybe I'll take a walk out around the place. Seems as if I'd like to be off by myself for a little while."

He went slowly down the side of the corn-patch till he reached the wild, unbroken prairie. A hot wind was stirring the grass, and shifting waves of brown and green swept over its surface, away and away to the horizon's rim. For long minutes he stood there, wanting to print the picture indelibly on his memory. He knew, now, that he would not see it again.

# SEVENTEEN

IN THE MORNING, WHEN HE HAD EATEN BREAKFAST, JONAthan saddled the tall roan. Uncle Ned watched him anxiously.

"You aimin' to leave, young Marse?" he asked at length.

"Yes," said the boy. "This place doesn't belong to me. I guess by law it goes to my father's widow—to Mrs. Brent. There's nothing to hold me here, now that he's gone."

"Yassuh," the old Negro nodded sadly. "Ah was hopin' Ah'd have white folks livin' on de place ag'in. Ain' got no other home."

"Why shouldn't you stay right here?" asked Jonathan. "If she took away her furniture when she left, it doesn't look as if she planned to come back. And if anybody ever does claim the farm, they'll probably be glad to have a hired man. Anyhow, you've got my permission to live here, for whatever it's worth."

The old man was almost tearful in his gratitude.

"Ef'n yo' ever come back dis way," he said, "Uncle Ned'll be wukkin' de place an' waitin' to make yo' welcome."

Jonathan thanked him and mounted. Then, on an impulse, he opened the pouch on his money belt and gave the old Negro two ten-dollar bills.

"That's for what you've done for my father and me," he said. "And I know you'll take care of his grave as long as you stay here."

He reined the horse around and rode away without a backward look. At Blue Prairie he entered the general store again. This time the proprietor himself was behind the counter. He was a thin, sallow-faced man with droopy black mustaches and a sour expression. He was civil enough to Jonathan, however, for the boy made several purchases and paid cash. As he transferred his flour and bacon to the saddlebag, Jonathan mentioned his father's name.

"Did you happen to know a man named Matthew Brent?" he asked.

"Yep. Sold him some nails an' stuff fer the house he was buildin'. Too bad he died like he did. Never even had a chance to git in one crop."

"Where did Mrs. Brent go—do you have any idea?"

"Oh, sure. She didn't hang 'round long after the buryin'. Less'n a week later a mover come through, headin' west. He was a widower with three young'uns an' needed a woman, so she went off with him the nex' day. Was you any kin to the Brents?"

"Yes," said Jonathan. "I'm a—a sort of relation. Well, I've got some traveling to do, an' I'd better get started."

"Come again," said the storekeeper, as the boy went out.

Jonathan swung into the saddle and turned his face eastward. He was eager to shake the dust of Blue Prairie from his feet. Spurring the big roan to a canter he was soon well away from the shoddy hamlet.

It was a cool, cloudy day—a good day for traveling. He was over the state line at nightfall, and made camp a few miles west of the Wabash. The next morning he crossed at Terre Haute. A signboard on a side road carried the name of Bloomington, and the boy paused, considering. It wouldn't be much out of his way to make a visit to the college town. He thought Noah Carter and his family must be well established there by now.

Moving steadily southeastward he reached a farmhouse in Monroe County only ten miles from his goal by suppertime that night. Fortified by a good night's sleep in a real bed and a hearty breakfast, he went out to saddle his horse. To his dismay he noticed that Doctor walked with a limp. The roan had been traveling hard and steadily for days on end, and on examination Jonathan saw that he had cast a front shoe.

He went back to the house and asked the farmer where the nearest blacksmith was to be found.

"Ain't none nearer'n West Forks—'bout five mile from here on the Bloomin'ton road," the man replied.

"All right," said Jonathan, "I can lead him that far. I'd rather go afoot than have a lame horse."

It was a hot morning and he went slowly, keeping to the soft ground along the roadside. Occasionally he stopped to let Doctor crop a few mouthfuls of grass. Two hours had passed and it was near the middle of the morning when he came in sight of the crossroads blacksmith shop.

A pair of work horses and a flea-bitten saddle mare were there ahead of him. He tied Doctor in the shade of a sycamore and watched the husky smith hammer out a shoe on the anvil. Two or three men lounged about under the trees. They eyed the stranger and his roan horse appraisingly, shot streams of tobacco juice into the dust, and talked local politics and crops.

An hour passed and the smith had the mare's left hind foot in his aproned lap, trimming the hoof for the final shoe, when Jonathan saw one of the loungers get up and stroll over toward Doctor. The man went close to the horse's withers as if measuring his height. As he turned away, Jonathan thought he caught a glance and a nod passing between the fellow and his companions. Then one of the others rose, stretched, and went down the side road beyond the smithy.

Their actions made the boy uneasy. He was glad when the blacksmith finished with the mare and announced that he was ready for the next job.

When Jonathan led Doctor in, there was a queer expression on the big man's face. He looked the roan over with narrowed eyes and made no move to pick up the horse's feet.

"It's the nigh front shoe," said the boy. "The one on the off foot is pretty well worn, too."

"Yeah," said the smith. "Mighty pretty saddle ye got there. Mexican work, ain't it? All that silver?"

"I guess so," Jonathan answered. "Don't know as I ever thought to ask where it was made."

The big fellow had shaped a new plate and was trying it on for size when a shadow darkened the wide door. Three men stood there—two of them the same loafers who had been sitting outside—the third a stout individual in a broad-brimmed hat, wearing a deputy sheriff's badge on his shirt front.

There was a moment while the law officer eyed the horse and the saddle, then shifted his beetling glance to Jonathan.

"Reckon ye're right, Bert," he said. "This is the feller."

He whipped out a murderous-looking horse pistol and pointed it at the boy's stomach.

"Don't ye make a move," he growled, "or I'll put a hole in ye bigger'n a peck basket. Search him fer weepons, boys."

For a moment Jonathan was too taken aback to open his mouth. Not until he had been relieved of his pocket pistol did he find words.

"G-gosh!" he said. "You must think I'm Rusty McKee! I'm not—I'm Jonathan Brent an' I can prove it. McKee's back in Sheldon's Grove, in jail."

The deputy shook his head. "Got ye dead to rights," he said. "Come out here an' have a look fer yerself."

Shoving the muzzle of the huge pistol into the boy's ribs he steered him toward a weather-stained handbill tacked to the wall of the blacksmith shop.

"Wanted for robbery and murder," Jonathan read. "Five hundred dollars' reward for the capture of the felon known as Rusty McKee. Height about 6 feet. Weight 160 pounds. Last seen riding a good roan horse, 16½ hands or over, white star in forehead, Mexican saddle inlaid with silver. This man is armed and dangerous."

"Won't deny that's the horse, will ye?" asked the deputy in triumph.

"No," said Jonathan, white-faced. "That's the horse McKee rode. But I've got a paper signed by the sheriff of Harley County—here, I'll let you read it."

Fumblingly he undid the pouch of his money-belt and handed over the folded sheet.

The stout man glanced at it and snorted. "Don't prove a thing," he said. "Likely ye stole it, along with the horse. I ain't givin' up a five-hundred-dollar reward that easy. Ye'll jest come with me to the justice o' the peace over to Bloomin'ton, an' see what he thinks o' yer story."

They waited while the blacksmith finished shoeing the roan and then set out. The deputy clambered aboard Doctor and settled his bulk in the handsome saddle.

"Looks faster'n any of our nags," he said. "I wouldn't trust this rascal not to try a git-away."

Jonathan mounted a sorry-looking old bay and the two loafers who had fetched the officer followed on their own horses.

It was an hour's ride into Bloomington. The boy had time to do some worrying, even though he was pretty sure the mistake would be cleared up. He watched the big roan's easy gait and felt proud of the way the horse carried his heavy rider.

A bell tolled the noon hour as they rode into the town

square. They tied the horses in front of a square frame house and the deputy sheriff knocked at the door. While they waited Jonathan read the small sign beside the doorframe: "Mordecai Peck, Justice of the Peace. Wills drawn up. Marriages performed."

Mr. Peck was a dried-up little man of sixty, with badly fitting false teeth. He came to the door with a napkin in his hand, evidently just risen from the dinner table.

"Ye'll have to wait," he snapped. "I'll talk to ye when I'm done eatin'. Set in there."

Jonathan and his captors went into the bleak little parlor and sat on slippery horsehair chairs for fifteen or twenty minutes. Nobody said a word. The boy's spirits got lower and lower.

Mr. Peck finally came in, wiping gravy off his shabby vest. "Well?" he asked sharply. "What seems to be the trouble here?"

The fat deputy got to his feet. "Reckon we've ketched that murderer everybody's talkin' about," he announced importantly.

He pulled the handbill out of his pocket and held it out with a flourish. "Take a look at his horse an' saddle."

Mr. Peck put on a pair of spectacles, read the description, then peered out the window.

"Could be the horse, right enough," he said. "Only 'tain't right to jump to conclusions. The judeecial mind has to weigh all the evidence. What ye got to say fer yer-self, young man?"

Jonathan swallowed and started to tell his story. "Mc-Kee stole the horse from a friend of mine—a painter named Tom Cole," he said. "I was driving for a blind man that sells books—Mr. Greenfield. Maybe you've heard of him. He's been out this far, other summers."

He went on to describe the attempted robbery of the old man and his capture of the bandit.

"I took 'em both to Sheldon's Grove, to the doctor's," he concluded. "Then Sheriff Evans turned the horse over to me with this paper."

The justice of the peace scanned the written words care-fully. "Seems to be all in order," said he. "Only one thing missin'. How ye goin' to prove yer name's Jonathan Brent? Without positive identification, this here paper ain't wuth a hoot."

The boy had a flash of inspiration. "I'll tell you who can identify me!" he exclaimed. "There's a professor at the college named Eliphalet Carter. I talked to his son, Noah, back in Pittsburgh. He'll remember me."

Mr. Peck nodded. "That ought to satisfy the law," he said. "Let me git my buggy hitched up an' we'll go out there."

It was an odd-looking cavalcade that proceeded along a dusty street toward the site of the new university. Squire

Peck rode first, holding the lines over a sleepy old white horse. The deputy came next on Doctor, with Jonathan following on the broken-down bay. And the two crossroads loungers brought up the rear.

Beyond the built-up section of the town, they passed a creek bend, half hidden by a clump of alders. A sound of splashing came from the water, and boys' voices were shouting and laughing. Jonathan looked longingly toward the swimming hole, for the noonday sun was hot.

At that moment the alder leaves parted and a freckled face peered up at the procession. "Hey!" yelled a voice that the Maine boy had heard before. "Hey, Jonathan Brent! Is that you?"

He reined in the horse and his escort stopped with him.

"Noah Carter!" he cried in return. "Gee, but I'm glad to see you!"

"Wait a jiffy," grinned the freckled lad. "I'm plumb naked, but I'll have some pants on in a couple o' seconds."

He dodged back out of sight and reappeared almost within the time limit he had set, pulling his galluses over one shoulder.

Mr. Peck was leaning out of his buggy and scowling. "What's all this?" he sputtered. "What you folks waitin' fer?"

Jonathan swung down out of the saddle and gripped his friend's hand. "You're just in time," he murmured. "They think I'm McKee, the robber. That fat fellow's a deputy sheriff an' he's getting ready to string me up."

Young Carter threw back his head and laughed. "I don't know what it's all about," he said. "But I'll do what I can to help. Who's the crotchety old party in the buggy?"

"Mr. Peck, the justice of the peace. Come an' tell him who I am."

They went forward together and faced the squire.

"Who be you?" asked Peck suspiciously.

"Noah Carter, sir. My father's professor of Greek at the University."

The little man nodded and got a firmer grip on his false teeth. "Carter, eh?" he said. "You 'quainted with this young feller?"

"Yes," Noah replied. "I met him coming west—on the Monongahela. He's from Maine and his name's Jonathan Brent."

"Ever hear of a man called McKee?" the squire shot back.

"Yes, sir. He robbed our steamboat captain in Pittsburgh and there was a good description of him posted. He's red-headed, forty years old an' better'n six feet tall."

Peck's eyes shifted to Jonathan and seemed to take stock of his age, height and color of hair.

"How 'bout the horse yonder—the big roan?" he asked next.

The Carter boy shook his head. "Mighty good-looking horse," he said. "But I never saw him before."

Meanwhile the stout deputy had ridden up. "Can't take a boy's evidence," he puffed in annoyance. "He ain't o' legal age."

The justice of the peace resented the interruption. "That's all ye know about the law," he snapped. "Looks to me like this whole thing is a piece o' foolishness. But to satisfy ye, we'll go on an' talk to the perfessor."

He took Noah with him in the buggy and they moved on. Eliphalet Carter's family occupied a new two-story house at the edge of the raw new campus.

He came out of his study in his shirt sleeves when Noah knocked at the door. His bow was courteous as he invited the whole group inside, but his long, studious face showed no sign of recognition when he glanced at Jonathan.

"Father," said Noah, "do you remember the little blind man selling books from a wagon, back in Pennsylvania?"

"Yes, yes," he replied in bewilderment. "Indeed I do. If I recall rightly I purchased a volume of Aristotle—"

"Sophocles, it was," Jonathan corrected him.

"Ah, yes," beamed the professor. "But how did you—oh, of course—it comes back to me now. You are the lad who assisted the gentleman—Mr. Greenfield, I believe his name was. Delighted to see you again, though I confess to being puzzled by the presence of such a—er, large delegation."

Noah chuckled. "This is Mr. Peck, our local justice of the peace," he said. "Maybe he'll explain."

A grimace that was meant for a smile twisted the squire's wrinkled face. "I don't reckon this needs to go any farther," he apologized. "Jest a durn fool mistake. Thank ye, perfessor, an' we'll be on our way. Deputy, give that boy his horse an' pistol an' take yer fat carcass back to the West Forks. Nex' time ye bring in a criminal, see to it ye've got more reason than in this here case."

# *EIGHTEEN*

JONATHAN HAD A GOOD SWIM IN THE CREEK WITH HIS FRIEND that afternoon, and spent the night at the Carters'. Next morning he made an early start eastward. In spite of Dr. Benton's assurance, he was worried about Nathaniel Greenfield. Rugged as he knew the old bookseller to be, a fractured skull was a dangerous injury for a man of his age.

The new front shoes had cured Doctor's limp, and the

big roan had had a good rest. He was eager to travel. They covered fifty miles that day and were well into Franklin County by suppertime the next evening. There was still an hour to sunset when Jonathan saw the name of Sheldon's Grove on a signpost, with the words "5 miles" beneath it. He pushed the big horse to a canter.

As he entered the Quaker village, Jonathan had a lump in his throat. These people had been very good to him. He wondered what they would think when he reappeared so soon. Up the street he saw the doctor's house and a small, plump figure with a bandaged head sitting in a rocker on the porch.

He swung out of the saddle and dropped the reins over a post. "Mr. Greenfield!" he called.

The little man turned his head quickly. "Jonathan?" he asked. "Can that really be you?"

The boy was up the porch steps at a bound. "That's right," he said. "I'm back again."

"Wait, now," smiled the bookseller. "Stand right there. I want to get a look at you."

"L-look at me?" Jonathan stammered.

"Yes," said the old man quietly. "A miracle has happened. That rascal did me a great favor when he hit me on the head. He gave me back my sight."

"Why, it's—it's wonderful," the boy gasped. "And you feel good, too? You're going to get well?"

"Practically well, this minute," Mr. Greenfield chuckled. "I'll be back on the road in a week, the doctor promises. You look just the way I'd imagined, Jonathan. A little bigger, perhaps, but the same honest face. What brings you back from Illinois so soon?"

Jonathan told him the whole unhappy tale. "I'm going back," he finished. "Maine is where I belong, I guess. I couldn't ever be content in a country without hills."

"Yes," the old man nodded. "I can remember what the Pennsylvania hills looked like in my youth—when the dogwood was in bloom. Besides, you're fond of your relatives back in Maine, I know. I'd like nothing better than your company on the van, but I sha'n't really need a driver now. Old Dolly and I can make out splendidly."

Samantha came to the front door just then and the doctor's chaise drove into the yard almost at the same moment. There was a general reunion before Jonathan stabled the horses and went in to supper.

That was a merry evening in the quiet Quaker household. Jonathan had all his adventures to recount, including his "capture" by the West Forks deputy.

"It was a mighty good thing I had that paper you got the sheriff to give me," he told Dr. Benton. "Where's McKee now? Still in jail, I hope."

"Yes," said the doctor. "But not here. The authorities came over from Ohio and took him back to stand trial for the Widow Peters' murder in Pickaway County. Sheriff Evans tells me he's got it fixed for thee to collect the reward, though. He was going to forward the money to thee in Illinois. Now thee can get it in person."

In the morning Jonathan paid a call at the sheriff's. The officer was at home and greeted him warmly.

"They're holdin' that reward fer ye down to Cincinnati," he said. "I hadn't sent 'em yer address yet. If ye're goin' that way, jes' drop in at the sheriff's office down there an' give 'em this note."

He sat down with pen and paper and produced another of his laborious scrawls.

"This will interduce the bearer as Jonathan Brent," it stated. "To my knowledge he is the one and only person who captured the robber and murderer McKee."

He signed the paper and added the county seal to give it a proper legal look.

After the noon meal, Jonathan said good-bye to the Bentons and his old employer, promising to write to all of them when he got back to the Maine farm. He camped a few miles north of Cincinnati that night and was riding into the city by ten the next morning. It was dog-days weather and the heat lay heavy in the valley under the bluff.

His first visit was to the courthouse, where the sheriff's office was located. Luckily he found the officer in and was able to deliver his note at once.

When he had read it, the sheriff pushed his spectacles back on his forehead and his eyes twinkled.

"Yep," he said, "Jake Evans told me all about you. I can see you're the lad from his description. Pretty plucky thing —bringin' in that desperado single-handed. The reward's yours, son. Just sign this receipt."

That was the end of the formalities. Jonathan walked out of the place with $500 in crisp new bills added to the amount he already carried in his money-belt.

All the way down from Sheldon's Grove he had been planning on how to get home the quickest way. Now that he had plenty of money he could afford to travel by steamboat, and his next call was at the waterfront.

There was a vessel due in from Louisville that afternoon, he learned, and she was scheduled to start up river in the evening.

"With the horse," the clerk told him, "the fare'll be fifty dollars to Pittsburgh. The *Columbine* ain't the biggest boat on the river but she's known as a flyer. High-pressure b'ilers an' a driver for a captain. Ought to make it in four days at the outside."

Jonathan paid the fare and received his stateroom ticket. On inquiry he found he would not be allowed to take the saddle to his stateroom with him. It was too valuable an article to be left exposed on the lower deck, where Doctor would be stabled, so the boy spent an hour or two shopping for a tack chest. He finally found what he wanted —a stout box with a padlock—and by the time he returned to the wharf the *Columbine* had tied up.

She was a medium-sized river steamer with the usual white-painted, fancy woodwork adorning her superstructure. Her skipper, a short, quick-moving Irishman with a red face and a powerful voice, stood on the "texas" forward of the pilot-house and bawled loud curses at the stevedores working below.

It was a proud moment for Jonathan when he watched a Negro deckhand lead the roan across the gangplank. On the lower deck aft, among bales of cotton and hogsheads of tobacco, there was room for two or three narrow stalls, and Doctor was tied in one of these. Jonathan had already stowed the silver-mounted saddle and bridle in the tack chest. He had it placed close to the horse's head, made sure that feed and water would be provided, and went up to his stateroom.

His quarters were somewhat disappointing. Even smaller than the cabin he had slept in aboard the *Phoebe Foster,* this one had a narrow bunk with a straw mattress and one tiny window. The name on the door was "New Hampshire." He was sorry it couldn't be "Maine," but the other state was at least a next-door neighbor.

Like all the other staterooms, this one opened directly off the main cabin—a long, narrow room with a bar at its forward end and a table running down the middle. Thinking he might go up to Mrs. Becker's boarding-house for supper, Jonathan asked the purser how soon the boat was likely to sail.

"Don't know for sure. But I'd stay aboard, if I was you," the man replied. "The ol' man's rushing the loading. He's got one eye on the bend, down river. The *Tennessee Belle's* due any minute, an' there'll be the devil to pay if we don't beat her to Pittsburgh."

Sure enough, the work was completed shortly after six, and the *Columbine* shoved off into the stream, smoke belching from her twin stacks, and her paddles threshing the water into foam. A triumphant hoot from her whistle turned all eyes astern. There, coming in toward the Cincinnati landing under full steam, was another steamboat—quite obviously the hated *Tennessee Belle.*

A few moments later Jonathan and his fellow passengers were called to supper. It was not a very tempting meal—tough boiled beef, cabbage, potatoes, cornbread and a wide variety of pickles and relishes. But to the country boy the way it was served seemed truly sumptuous. The white cloth on the table, the silver and china and the black waiters bowing and scraping, made a setting such as he had hardly imagined.

After sunset he sat on the little railed afterdeck and watched the forested banks slip astern into the dark. It was a big, wild country, with only an occasional settlement scratched out of the wilderness. The deck was protected by a wooden overhead canopy, and he could hear sparks and cinders dropping on it when fresh cordwood was fed to the fires.

Before he went to bed the *Columbine* steered in to a wood-landing on the Kentucky shore, and for half an hour the sweating Negroes heaved oak and pine aboard. Then the engine bell rang and the paddles churned into action once more. The vibration of the boat kept Jonathan awake for an hour or two, but when he finally got used to the throbbing, it lulled him to sleep.

It was full daylight when the seven o'clock breakfast call roused him next morning. He hurried into his clothes, washed at the outdoor basin provided on the forward deck, and got to the table in time to partake of ham and eggs and fried potatoes.

The lady passengers stayed in their staterooms most of the day. Some of the men drank whisky at the bar or played poker at tables in the cabin. The day was another hot, sultry one and even sitting still, Jonathan found he was drenched with perspiration. He went down once or twice to make certain Doctor was getting proper attention. It was actually cooler there than up in the staterooms, for a solid pile of cargo in front of the stalls served to cut off the heat from the boilers.

On one of his trips below, Jonathan went forward to take a look at the clanking engine. He felt sorry for the men who stoked the fires, the sweat pouring in streams down their naked black backs. But they appeared to mind it very little. They sang and chuckled mightily as they flung open the red-hot doors and hurled big chunks of wood into the flames.

A violent thundershower broke the heat about the time they tied up at Portsmouth that afternoon. The stop there was a short one and they were on their way again by three o'clock. The captain, whose name, Jonathan discovered, was Riordan, still kept a watchful eye on the river astern and never allowed the pressure to go down in the boilers. But it was not until they were leaving Marietta, on the third morning, that the *Tennessee Belle* came into view again.

The pursuing steamer must have had very little cargo to land, for she barely touched the landing. Two or three passengers could be seen running up the gangplank, then it was jerked back aboard and the big white craft swung out into the *Columbine's* wake.

There was a roar of profanity from the texas. "More steam down there!" yelled Captain Riordan. "Stoke that fire! Tie down that safety valve! Get her rarin'!"

The fire doors clattered, the pistons hissed louder and the walking-beam began bucking up and down at quickened speed. Under the flailing paddles the river fled behind them in a surge of turbulent white.

That was a race to remember. The passengers caught the contagion of the affair and spent the whole day in a fever of excitement. Even the ladies jumped up and down on the afterdeck and screamed encouragement to their craft. When the *Tennessee Belle* pushed her sharp nose abreast of the *Columbine's* stern, sneaking up on the inside of a bend, three female passengers fainted and had to be revived with smelling salts.

The rival boat ran out of fuel first and dropped behind a good three miles while taking on wood. But by noon it was the *Columbine's* turn to put in at a landing. The passengers watched in anguished silence while the *Belle* swept past. Some of the men, with Jonathan among them, even jumped ashore and helped handle wood with the deckhands. They cut the loading time to a bare fifteen minutes, and were back in the race once more.

There was a ringing cheer when they entered a four-mile straight stretch of river and caught sight of the other boat far ahead. Before she disappeared around another bend they knew they had gained nearly a mile, and wagering languished because few were willing to bet against the *Columbine*.

Jonathan listened to the furiously laboring engine and wondered whether the machinery could stand it. Old-time

COLUMBINE

THAT WAS A RACE TO REMEMBER

river travelers aboard had already begun talking about boiler explosions.

"Why," said one smiling gentleman, "it was only two years ago that Riordan got in a race with the *Shawnee.* He was skipper o' the *Western Star* then. When the pressure got too high he slung a bull chain over the safety valve an' had the biggest man in the crew hangin' on the end of it. He was ahead an' gainin' when the boilers let go. Just west o' Paducah, that was. Twenty-two passengers lost."

The *Columbine* wooded up again about sunset and roared ahead into the darkness, her stacks shooting red sparks skyward. Wheeling was just ahead on the east bank, and they saw the *Tennessee Belle* veering in to make a landing. All the passengers were gathered on the texas now, and they howled with delight. The *Columbine,* they knew, carried no freight for Wheeling.

Jonathan left the cheering crowd and went aft to the companionway. He could feel the deck shudder under his feet, and while he knew little about steamboats, he had an uneasy feeling about this one. Quietly he went down to stand beside Doctor.

The big roan had been calm enough through the earlier part of the voyage. Now he snorted and his eyes rolled, showing the whites. Under Jonathan's soothing hand his sleek hide trembled. He was sweating, though the air was cool.

The explosion came with a rending, deafening roar and a shock that threw the boy flat on the deck. His wind was knocked out and he lay there straining to get the air back into his lungs. There was a terrible sound of screaming somewhere forward. Then, as Jonathan struggled to his feet, the bow belched out a roaring sheet of flame. In the fierce glow of the blaze and the smothering smoke, he wrenched the key from his pocket and unlocked the tack chest. Doctor was rearing and jerking at the halter rope and it was all the boy could do to throw the saddle on his back and pull up the cinch. With fumbling fingers he undid the halter. There was no time to put on the bridle. He scrambled for the left stirrup, hauled himself into the saddle and drove a heel hard into Doctor's heaving side.

Out of the corner of his eye, Jonathan saw a flaming cotton-bale toppling down on them. But the big horse whirled in time. At a single leap he cleared the rail and soared out over the black water.

# *NINETEEN*

THE BOY WAS LIFTED CLEAR OF THE SADDLE AS THEY HIT THE river. He went under, still clinging to the halter rope, and came up after a second or two, blowing water out of his mouth and nose. The roan was swimming strongly toward the Virginia shore. Jonathan pulled himself forward by the rope till he could get a firm grip on the horse's mane.

Behind them the whole river was lit by a terrifying red glare. He looked back and saw black figures jumping from the blazing deck and superstructure of the steamer. A boat, launched from the Wheeling landing, shot past him with a frantic splash of oars. He saw others following and thought dully that the survivors who had reached the river would be picked up.

The whole disaster had come so suddenly that the boy's mind was still numb. For the moment he could neither feel the horror of what had happened nor realize the miracle of his escape. It was as if he struggled through the vague awfulness of a nightmare from which he could not wake.

Then he felt Doctor's forefeet take hold on the muddy bottom close to shore. The big horse floundered toward the steep bank, gathered his powerful haunches under him and went up with a rush, pulling Jonathan after him. Dripping and trembling, the roan stood on solid ground, his sides heaving like a blacksmith's bellows.

Jonathan was crouched on the bank, staring dazedly at the river, when the *Columbine* sank. There was a great hiss of steam, a last uprush of sparks, and then utter blackness. The boy shivered and straightened up. Behind him the roan snorted. A soft, wet muzzle rubbed against his arm impatiently.

"Good ol' Doctor!" Jonathan murmured, with a choke

in his voice. He felt along the horse's side and found the saddle hanging askew by its loosened girth. While he was straightening it and hauling the strap tight he could hear voices coming over the water.

"Got 'em all?"

"Yeah—I reckon. How many'd you pick up?"

"Seven."

"Nine here. Must ha' been more—plenty more—got burnt or drownded."

"Some o' these are in bad shape. We're takin' 'em ashore."

"Yeah—no use lookin' 'round out here any more."

Suddenly Jonathan was sick. When he finished retching he staggered to Doctor's side and hoisted himself into the saddle. He wanted to get away from there.

Fortunately, it was a comfortable July night. Jonathan's dripping clothes dried fast as the roan jogged northward along the river road, and he felt no chill. They passed through sleeping villages where dogs roused to bark at them, and through stretches of overhanging woods where owls hooted eerily. It was nearing dawn and they had put almost a score of miles behind them when Jonathan guided the horse into a field. There was a big stack of new wheat straw there. He tied the end of the halter rope around his wrist and tumbled into the straw, asleep almost before he lay down.

The sun was up when a gentle tug at the rope woke him. Doctor stood there munching straw and eying him with mild reproof. The boy got up groggily and stretched his stiff arms and legs. The memory of the night before came back to him and he felt weak. But he gritted his teeth and shook off the horror of it.

Before mounting again he examined his money-belt and found it intact, with the bills dry in their buckskin pouch. His saddlebags were gone—for they had been in the stateroom aboard the *Columbine.* The little pistol had to have its wet charge drawn, and as he had no dry powder he left it unloaded in his pocket.

Half an hour later, he rode into the little town of Wellsburg. There was a general store at the first street corner and he went in and bought some bread and cheese and half a sack of oats. Then he fed Doctor and sat on the step eating his own breakfast.

One or two passers-by stared at the horse curiously. The fine saddle went strangely with the rope halter, he had to admit. When he had swallowed the last dry mouthful he went across the street to a harness-maker's shop and asked to see a bridle. The gray-haired little German who owned the place had nothing but work and driving harness on hand. But he offered to put together a light bridle with a plain bar bit for four dollars. Jonathan led the roan over and let the old craftsman make measurements of his head. Then he watched while the leather was carefully cut and stitched.

He had been there perhaps an hour when the hoot of a steamboat whistle came up from the river. Townspeople went hurrying down to the wharf at the foot of the street. The arrival of a steamer was evidently a big event in Wellsburg. Two or three minutes later there was a pounding of feet in the dusty road outside, and a small boy stuck his head in at the door.

"Ye heard the news?" he panted. "Steamboat blew her b'ilers, down to Wheelin'. More'n forty people kilt!"

The old German shrugged his shoulders. "Ach–shteamboats! Vy should beeples ride on dem t'ings!"

Shivering a little, Jonathan wondered too.

By the time the crowd began straggling up from the landing the bridle was finished. Doctor champed at the new bit, christened it with a long drink at the village watering-trough, and settled down to traveling once more. There was a trail heading eastward over the hills toward Pittsburgh, forty miles away. Jonathan decided to take it instead of the river road. The sooner he put the Ohio behind him the better he would feel.

The country was rough and wild. In a dozen miles he passed only two or three cabins, standing desolately in little clearings. Late in the afternoon he came to a tumble-down tavern and stopped for a meal. The bearded innkeeper peered at him out of mean little red-rimmed eyes and said there wouldn't be anything to eat till suppertime. Then he glanced at the silver-mounted saddle and his expression changed to one of crafty interest.

"I dunno," he said. "Come to think of it, I got a fire goin' an' I could put a hunk o' sidemeat on to fry. Ye better stay the night. I can fix ye up a bed. It's bad country on beyond."

Jonathan was hungry, but he didn't like the man's looks. He pulled his belt a notch tighter and rode off, with the tavernkeeper's curses ringing in his ears. A mile farther on he stopped at a mountain stream, where he baited the roan with grain and tried to ease the ache in his own stomach with a big drink of water.

It grew cold after sunset and he had no blanket. There was nothing to do but keep on riding. He gave Doctor his head and the good horse plodded along the dark trail hour after hour. That was a miserable night. Jonathan had to ride crouched forward in the saddle to shield his face from low-hanging branches. Once or twice he fell asleep and was only wakened by the brushing of leaves against his head or the scream of a wildcat off in the woods. Cold, famished and lonesome, he clung to the saddle and waited for daylight.

When the sky finally began to gray, he heard roosters crowing and knew he was nearing a settlement of some kind. Cleared ground and cornfields appeared along the trail. At last, just before sunrise, he came to a good-sized farmhouse and saw a man going out to the barn carrying milk pails.

He hitched the tired horse in the yard and climbed down stiffly. The farmer turned at the barn door and looked him over with a good-natured grin.

"Where'd you come from, young feller?" he asked. "Look sort o' tuckered out."

"Guess I am," Jonathan replied, smiling wanly. "I rode over from Wellsburg. Suppose I could get some breakfast?"

"You sure can. Ought to be ready pretty quick. Jes' go to the kitchen an' my ol' woman'll fix you up."

Ten minutes later the boy was reveling in eggs, sausage, buckwheat cakes and sorghum molasses. He got up from the table feeling like a new man.

At his insistence the housewife accepted half a dollar for the meal. But she wouldn't hear of his going until he had rested.

"Give your horse some hay, an' go take a nap in the barn," she told him. Her husband, returning from his milking, backed up her invitation, and Jonathan gave in.

He slept till nearly noon, and stayed for dinner with the hospitable couple. Then he gave Doctor a much-needed grooming. It was well along in the afternoon when he rode into Pittsburgh and stabled the horse at a down-town hotel. For a dollar he got a small room on the third floor.

When he looked into the cracked mirror over the washbasin he realized what a sight he was. The shirt in which he had escaped from the burning steamer was grimy and wrinkled and his hair was so tangled he could hardly get a comb through it. Making himself as presentable as he could he went out to try to get some clothes.

A tailor in the next block had haberdashery on display, and Jonathan bought a couple of shirts, a change of underwear and socks and a secondhand jacket. He was coming out with his purchases under his arm when he noticed a huddle of people around a store window next door. For a moment he couldn't see what they were looking at, but he could hear some of their comments.

"Jest as nat'ral as life, ain't it?"

"That's my house yonder. I kin see the chim'ley."

"What's the boat at the landin'? *Tennessee Belle?*"

"Shucks, no! That's the *Tuscarora.* Cain't ye read the name, top o' the pilot-house?"

Jonathan edged in till his nose was close to the small-paned window. Enough daylight shone in above the heads of the crowd for him to see a large canvas on an easel. The painting glowed with the golden color of afternoon. It had been made somewhere high on the bluff behind the town and showed a broad view of the river, the steamboats and other craft, and the stores, warehouses and dwellings of Pittsburgh. Stooping a little, the boy made out the neatly lettered signature in a lower corner: "Th. Cole."

Quickly he elbowed his way out of the throng and tried the door of the shop. It was unlocked. He hurried inside and came face to face with the proprietor, an elderly stationer with a bunch of keys in his hand. The man peered at him severely through steel-bowed spectacles.

"Can't do any more business today, young man. I'm about to lock up," he said.

"It's about Tom Cole," Jonathan told him breathlessly. "The artist who painted that picture in the window. Can you tell me where he is?"

"Hmm—yes. Cole. Of course. Let me see—I think he said he was staying at Bassett's boarding-house. It's up the street there, two or three blocks away."

The boy thanked him and rushed out. Five minutes later he had located Bassett's and was asking about his friend.

"Reckon he's up in his room, messin' with them paints," the sour-faced mistress of the house informed him. "Second floor back."

At Jonathan's knock a deep, pleasant voice told him to come in. Tom Cole looked up from his easel and his eyebrows lifted quizzically. For a moment he didn't recognize his visitor. Then a sudden grin of delight overspread his face.

"You're Nat Greenfield's driver!" he exclaimed. "Jonathan—that's it—Jonathan Brent. I thought you'd be way out in Illinois before this!"

Quickly the boy poured out his story. "I guess you didn't get my letter—the one I sent to New York," he said. "But anyhow, I've got your horse, all safe an' sound. An' McKee's in jail, ready to be tried for murder."

The painter slapped his thigh, delighted at the news. "I'd given up hope of ever seeing Duke again," he cried. "Duke was my name for the roan. That scoundrel stole him while I was painting a sunset, up the Monongahela. I had the horse tied in a thicket, and the place I was working was only a hundred feet away. When I went back he'd disappeared. But you say you caught McKee? And that pistol really did some good?"

Jonathan described the shooting and how he had taken his prisoner and the old bookseller to the doctor's.

"But the best part of all," he concluded, "is that Mr. Greenfield can see again. Next time you meet him he'll be driving himself!"

"Wonderful!" the artist beamed. "What a lucky day it was for the old gentleman when he met you! Come on—I want to see the horse, and I'll buy you a supper."

When they reached the hotel stable, Cole went into the stall to stroke the roan. He complimented Jonathan on the horse's condition.

"Maybe Doctor's a better name for him after all," he grinned. "This Dr. Benton must be quite a man. I want to meet him some day. And I see you've even got the saddle! That's a surprise, because it's worth two or three hundred dollars. I thought the thief would have sold it long ago. That's a new bridle though, isn't it?"

Hesitantly, Jonathan told him about the *Columbine*. Some of the horror of the thing had left him now, but it was still hard for him to talk about it. The artist understood.

"I'd heard the news," he nodded soberly. "The *Tennessee Belle* came in this morning. Thank God the horse got you out!"

They had supper together at the hotel. It was a good meal and Jonathan told more of his adventures, listening in turn while Cole recounted some of his own.

"I've shipped most of my canvases East," he said, "and I'll be starting back to New York in a month or so. What do you plan to do now?"

"Head for Maine the shortest way," the boy grinned. "I've plenty of money for the trip and I aim to go right through to Philadelphia by canal and railroad. From there it shouldn't be too hard to get passage on a ship, at least as far as Boston. And once I'm in Boston I'd be willing to walk the rest o' the way!"

After supper Jonathan turned over the big roan to his rightful owner and watched them trot away up the street. Some day he hoped to see both horse and rider again, for Cole had promised before he left that he would come to Maine and paint the Kennebec.

In the morning the boy booked passage on one of the boats of the "Pioneer" Line, and before nightfall he was traveling eastward toward the mountains—not as a stowaway this time, but proudly established in the cabin as a paying passenger!

# TWENTY

JONATHAN GOT OFF THE TRAIN IN PHILADELPHIA, FIVE DAYS after leaving Pittsburgh. It was late afternoon when he descended from the dusty coach and combed the cinders out of his hair.

As soon as he got his bearings he started walking down Market Street toward the Delaware River. He could see the water at the foot of the wide thoroughfare, and the tall masts of shipping, moored along the docks. It was a big, busy town, though less of a beehive than New York. There was something solid about the brick office buildings that he liked. And Philadelphia, he was glad to see, kept its hogs at home.

He was crossing Front Street and starting down the steeper slope to the riverfront when he became aware of two people a little distance ahead of him. There were dozens of others on the street, but this particular couple aroused his interest. One was a stocky man of middle height, with a roll to his walk and a fringe of gray curls showing beneath the back of his sea-faring cap. His companion was a slim young woman, in a blue silk gown, which she held up daintily with one hand to keep the hem of her skirt out of the dust.

Jonathan quickened his pace, hardly realizing that he did so. For some reason he could not explain, he wanted to hear their voices.

They were chatting gaily. He caught the girl's merry laugh and then some words spoken by the gray-haired man. "I swan, Prue—'tain't fair to make a mock o' yer old man like that."

Jonathan's heart gave a jump. "Swan" was a Maine word, and that was a Maine man's voice and inflection. He hurried on till he came abreast of them.

"Cap'n Foster!" he gasped. "Cap'n Foster an' Miss Prudence!"

They stopped in mid-stride, staring at him as if he had

been an apparition. Then the girl burst into a ringing peal of laughter.

"Don't you recognize him, Father?" she asked. "It's Jonathan—Jonathan Brent from Cobbosseecontee! Oh—I'm sorry I laughed at you, Jonathan, but such a dirty face I never saw!"

The boy's face grew hot with shame, and he snatched a none-too-clean handkerchief from his pocket. It was nearly black after a wipe or two at his cheeks.

"G-gosh!" he stammered. "It must have been the train. I—I just got off an' haven't had a chance to wash."

Prudence caught his arm with an impulsive hand. "You come right down to the *Phoebe Foster* with us!" she cried. "You can slick up all you want. And please forgive me. I didn't mean to hurt your feelings. But it *was* funny!"

Captain Foster lifted his cap and scratched his head in puzzlement. "How in creation did ye get back here to Philadelphy, son?" he asked.

"It's a pretty long story," Jonathan smiled. "The main thing is that I'm not going to live in the West. I'm going back to the Kennebec."

"Honest? Well, then—by the great bull whale—ye're sailin' home with us!"

He hit Jonathan a tremendous clap on the back and took his other arm. Thus escorted, the boy crossed the waterfront cobbles and soon reached the wharf where the schooner lay. Her clean paint and taut rigging looked smart as a new-minted dollar in the light of the setting sun. When he stood on deck and looked up at the tall, straight masts of Maine pine, he felt a choking lump in his throat.

. . .

The *Phoebe Foster* sailed next day with a cargo of sail-cloth from Philadelphia looms, and saws and axes from Philadelphia forges. She made a slow voyage down the Delaware, tacking against a light south wind. But once outside the Capes she bowled along at a good clip with the breeze on her quarter.

Jonathan took a hand at the ropes whenever a chance offered. Most of the men in the crew were the same ones he had sailed with in the spring. They remembered him and welcomed him back. The captain, however, refused to assign him to a watch. He was a guest, the burly skipper insisted.

So it was that he had long, pleasant hours to spend with Prudence, fishing with handlines over the taffrail or spinning yarns about his westward journey as they sat in the shadow of the mainsail.

"You've grown up, Jonathan," she told him once. "You're not a shy country boy any more. You've learned to think and act for yourself. I liked you before, but I believe I like you better this way."

He looked straight into her eyes to make sure she wasn't

teasing him. "That's right," he said. "I feel about ten years older. And yet it's only been three months since I left the farm."

"Do your uncle and aunt know you're on the way home?" she asked.

He shook his head. "I thought I'd write from Cincinnati, but then I got passage on the boat and figured I'd be there as quick as a letter. I hope they won't be very upset by my coming back."

She smiled a little. "I wouldn't worry too much about that," she said.

The weather held fair. On the fourth day out they were making a long reach across the Gulf of Maine. And on the morning of the fifth they headed up between the islands at the mouth of the Kennebec.

There was a nip in the air. "After all," thought Jonathan, "it's August. Might get a touch of frost any time now."

He drew a deep breath of the invigorating air and watched the whitecaps dance at the entrance to Merrymeeting Bay.

They tied up at Richmond Wharf that afternoon and discharged part of their cargo. With the early morning tide they were on their way up the river, and shortly after noon Gardiner was in sight.

"Well," said Prudence soberly, "here's the end of the

voyage. When do you suppose I'll see you again, Jonathan?"

He liked the way she said it. "I can tell you one thing," he answered. "It won't be so long this time. Why don't you drive up and pay us a visit at the farm? I'd like to show you Cobbossee."

She nodded. "I was thinking the same thing. And how about your coming down to see me?"

"I promise," said he, and they shook hands on that.

Going ashore was a simple matter for Jonathan. He had no luggage except a little bundle of spare linen. He said his good-byes and tried again to pay the skipper for his passage, but Captain Foster was firm.

"Get along with ye, now," he urged. "I'd give a pine tree shillin' to see Eli's face when ye walk in."

The boy got a ride on a farm wagon up the river road to Hallowell. There he climbed the long hill and started the last five miles on foot. Every farmhouse and field, every stone wall and elm tree was familiar to him now. His heart felt light and he walked and ran by turns without tiring.

It was nearing six o'clock when he reached the "Forks." The crossroads was deserted at that hour. The general store and blacksmith shop had closed for the day, and curls of smoke from supper fires rose above the chimneys. Jonathan hurried on up Meeting House Hill, craning his neck for a first glimpse of the lake.

There it was at last—a sheet of gold in the sunset, glimmering through the pines. He felt like singing as he went over the crest of the hill.

The farm lay peaceful on its hillside. He could see the Astrakhans and Summer Sweetings ripening in the apple orchard, where the lambs grazed—as big as their mothers now. The cattle were gathered at the foot of the lane waiting to be milked.

Jonathan tiptoed up the porch steps. Through the window he could see Uncle Eli's back and Aunt Polly's gentle face, where they sat at the table. He lifted the door-latch, trying not to make a noise.

"Hello, folks," he called softly. "It's Jonathan. I'm home!"

Inside there was the quick scrape of a chair pushed back. He heard Aunt Polly's breathless voice—"Eli! Could it be—"

Then he flung the door wide, and the next moment their arms were around him.

. . .

Half an hour later he was still eating, still answering questions.

"Aunt Polly," he laughed, "if I sat here and told you all that's happened it would be midnight before I got through. Those cows are getting mighty unhappy out there. I promise, when the chores are done, I'll tell the whole story from start to finish. But right now I want to find out if I've forgotten how to milk. Come on, Uncle Eli—let's get to work!"

His old barn boots stood in their accustomed place in the shed outside the kitchen door. They felt good to his feet. He went out across the lawn, where the first drops of dew were forming, and opened the gate that let the cows come down to the barnyard. As they moved forward in stately procession, he turned his face to the sunset breeze and filled his lungs with a deep draught of Maine's own air. From somewhere down in the woods by the lake came a sound like a benediction—the liquid, haunting bell-notes of a hermit thrush.

He was home.

www.ingramcontent.com/pod-product-compliance
Lightning Source LLC
Chambersburg PA
CBHW020552310726
48979CB00008B/1190/J

* 9 7 8 1 9 3 1 1 7 7 1 2 2 *